Damien's

Secret

SUNNI T. CONNOR

DEDICATION

I dedicate this book to my beautiful family and my
loyal readers. Special thanks to my children for
showing unconditional love. Thanks to my parents
for allowing me to be the unique individual I am.
Thanks to my soul mate for completing my soul.
Lastly, thanks to my readers because there would be
no books to be read without you.

TABLE OF CONTENTS

ACKNOWLEDGMENTS

Published by Naturally Sunni LLC.

1
DAMIEN

I'm Damien, well, so I thought. My entire life, as I knew it was a mystery. Many people wondered what happened to me that screwed me up so bad. Only two people actually knew the truth, one was dead, and one couldn't expose the truth without exposing himself. No one wanted to face what happened, and I didn't even know how it happened. Things spiraled out of control so rapidly. I couldn't comprehend how I lost so much of myself just to hide a secret. How did my one lie turn into a life full of lies? I often wondered what shifted in my life that caused things to go from normal to a complete catastrophe.

I tried to keep my composure, and everything was good until I made the ultimate mistake that changed everything. It was the mistake that changed the entire direction of my fate. It would haunt me and keep me forever enslaved in my own skin. I couldn't escape who I was, and I surely couldn't run from my secret. My secret was a part of me, like every grain of hair that sat on my head. It was that attached. It walked how I walked, and it patiently waited to be exposed. All secrets come to light. What's done in the dark will eventually be revealed.

I was an attractive thirteen-year-old boy when everything fell apart. My brown caramel skin was flawless. Every feature on my face had a place, enhancing my look. The grain of my hair was curly. No one ever saw my wide, fluffy curls. Papa made me get a military-style haircut every week. He never paid me much mind, but he always ensured I got a haircut. A haircut that I despised.

My eyes favored a cat. They had a specific shape which caused a look some would never forget. I had a mole on my face which stood out. I was slim but not skinny. I cared about my appearance, unlike most thirteen-year-old boys. Everything had to match and fit perfectly. I'd change my clothes 20 times until my outfit met my expectations. My demanding ways annoyed my mother. I was a weird freak about my teeth. I forcefully brushed them at least twice a day.

There I stood in the bathroom, trying to hold my chest up straight and brush my teeth rough like I had seen my handsome father do on many occasions. My father, well, we called him Papa, was a tall, handsome man, he was noticeably attractive, but he had a drunk face. His eyes were more creme-colored than white. He wasn't at the yellow drunken eyes stage, but he was on his way. His hair was never cut, but he had lovely curls that enhanced his milky brown skin. Although he was a drunk, it didn't stop the fact that he was extremely attractive.

All the neighborhood women flirted, and he sneakily helped them with their grocery bags. Sometimes he wouldn't come back out of their homes for hours. Maybe he helped them cook too. Papa was a part-time dad. He only came around once or twice a week, but he claimed to live with us. Every Friday, like clockwork, he would appear on Mama's payday to fuck her, cut off all my curls, eat dinner and spend her money getting drunk. Mama loved Fridays.

I glanced at my eyes in the bathroom mirror, and I admired the glassy look that reflected back to me. I felt my eyes made me unique. My eyes knew all the answers. You can't look in your eyes and lie to yourself. It's almost impossible. You see the world through your sight, and it holds all your truths. All people like to see something special in themselves; well, I was no different. I jumped out of my daze as I heard Mama's voice aggressively calling me. Maybe it wasn't her first time calling me. I wouldn't know because I was in a deep daydream. Mama bitched so much that I often ignored her. It was always something wrong or something I had to do. Her nagging drove me insane.

Mama was a fox. She was so beautiful, but she seemed unaware of her beauty. She matched Papa well in the look department. He was a catch, and so was she. Mama had pretty full hair that she wore in an afro state. Her lashes seemed to come out past her nose. People everywhere complimented her long eyelashes. Her body was fit as if she didn't have any kids at all. Her teeth were perfect, and she didn't have one noticeable flaw.

Mama seemed to ignore her beauty. She seemed oblivious of how attractive she was. She just focused on working and being a wife. She usually wore work clothes, but she cleaned up well on occasion when she actually had something to do. Mama was the loving type of mother before Papa became a drunk. If Papa was happy, then Mama was happy, and then we could be happy. Everything revolved around Papa. We ate many cold dinners waiting for Papa to come home. Sometimes, he never came home, and Mama would look disappointed every time.

I couldn't understand why she wouldn't leave him. Why was she so afraid to be alone. She could clearly get any man she wanted. Time after time, she chose to be Papa's option. She was his wife, and she should never be an option. The way Papa treated Mama made me hate him. He didn't particularly care for me either. I was the only one in the house who complained about Papa. Mama didn't want to hear the truth.

I heard Mama scream my name again. I didn't rush to answer her. I never ran to do anything. I slowly put the lid on the toothpaste; I grabbed the toothbrush and placed it in the holder as I wiped the excess spit from around my mouth. I hummed as I hung the face towel on the side of the sink.

"Damien! Boy, I know you hear me calling you. If you make me walk up these steps!" Mama yelled from the bottom of the steps.

"I'm coming, Ma. Sorry I was brushing my teeth," I calmly stated, unbothered by all her yelling.

"Why do you spend all that damn time in the bathroom anyway? You are not a …" Mama stopped mid-sentence.

"I'm not a what, Mama?" I asked with more aggression in my voice.

"Nevermind, Damien. Just get your ass down here, so I can go to work. Dawn never gives me this much trouble," Mama stated as she slammed the front door.

"I'm not Dawn!" I screamed to the already shut door.

Dawn was my beautiful twin sister. I liked to call her Danny Girl. It was my personal nickname for her. We were strangely identical twins. Usually, different-sex twins don't look as much alike as Dawn and I. We didn't differ much at all. We had the same complexion, head shape, lip shape, nose, height, and weight. Dawn, however, didn't have my perfectly-shaped eyes. She had a slant but not like mines. Dawn was my father's favorite, and recently, she became my mother's favorite too.

I loved Dawn, and we shared a special bond. After all, she was my twin. Having a twin is like being the same person. We shared our mother's womb at the same time, we grew up in the exact same grade, we liked all the same food, and we even had the same favorite color. Dawn has always been a bit more quiet and submissive. I challenged everything, Dawn challenged nothing, but she enjoyed annoying me.

Dawn sat at the kitchen table drinking the leftover cereal milk from the bowl with an obnoxious slurping sound. I glanced at her and smiled. She shied away. I hate when she does that. She knows that annoys me. I like to be acknowledged when I enter a room, and she knows that. So, she purposely ignored me every morning.

"What the hell was wrong with Mama this morning?" I asked while looking in the refrigerator for the milk.

"She's mad Daddy left in the middle of the night again. You can stop looking for the milk. I drank the last of it," Dawn replied with a sneaky smirk.

"Danny Girl, why do you love to get me upset? I told you I would be nice if you were nice. Do you remember?" I asked in a calm, subtle tone.

"Yeah, Damien, I remember. I just didn't want you to think you were about to eat a bowl of cereal, that's all," she replied as she picked up her book bag and walked towards the front door.

"Everyone around here takes everything from me. I share everything with you, and you couldn't even save me some milk?" I yelled as I blocked her from opening the front door.

"Come on, Damien. Stop being a baby and move from in front of the door. There's no need to get upset. I love you. Now move your foot and let me go to school," Dawn stated nicely as she grabbed the doorknob.

"Perfect little Dawn, always have the right answers. Sure, I'll move my foot and let you go to school. I'll be right behind you, okay," I said as I moved a piece of Dawn's hair behind her ear. The hair was out of place. I was obsessed with Dawn's hair. It was the one thing she had that I didn't. Her hair was long and full but often out of place. I then removed my foot and watched her walk off the porch. I stood in the doorway and counted the four steps as Dawn quickly jumped them. 1, 2, 3, 4, and there she goes, I counted in my mind.

I slowly shut the door and locked it. I opened the refrigerator and pulled out a secret department at the bottom. I removed the potatoes and slid out a half-gallon of milk that I had hidden. I grabbed a bowl and a spoon and sat in Dawn's favorite seat. I poured the cereal, then the milk, and I crunched quietly as I tapped my right foot up and down. In silence, I got lost in my thoughts. I peacefully ate my cereal as I mocked Dawn. I pretended I was her. I moved my imaginary hair out of my face. I talked aloud in Dawn's voice as if I was talking to her best friend, Brianna.

I don't know why I enjoyed role-playing. I got a real thrill out of being Dawn. I always felt if I could understand her, I wouldn't lose her. I admired the way she walked; her legs were strong but light. Her tiny delicate feet touching the floor was always soft as a petal. She moved with a feathery flop as if she was always happy to walk to her next destination. I'm a boy, so my walk and posture were more solid. I'm not sure why I admired Dawn so much. We were close to the same; the only difference was, she was delicate, and I was solid.

I left the house and turned the lock behind me. The

moment the Detroit air hit my face, I knew I had to be aware of my surroundings. I stuck my chest out and walked with my head held high. My neighborhood was a decent place with a little violence and minor drug selling. It wasn't a neighborhood full of hood guys who stood around drinking and smoking weed all day, but there were the occasional urban problems. We rarely heard gunshots, but if we did, it was usually coming from blocks away. Mostly, the old heads ran the neighborhood, and they sat at the barbershops or outside the liquor store playing chess. They talked trash all day about how completely screwed up the world was.

I was cool with everyone in the neighborhood except for one man named Mr. Ralph. He happened to be one of Papa's close friends. I just didn't like the way he looked at me. Mr. Ralph was a tall slinky man, he had holes in his face, and his lips were thin with a mixture of pink and brown. I despised the sight of his lips. He always watched me walk to school. Every morning I walked alone. Dawn always went to school early for band practice.

Mr. Ralph would stare at me like a distant owl. An owl that sits in the shadow to avoid exposure. It was the most uncomfortable feeling. I tried to walk harder to let him know I wasn't scared. I Bopped harder, and I even mugged him when we caught eye contact. He smiled every single time.

Mr. Ralph had a nephew, or maybe it was his son. His name was Brandon. He lived with Mr. Ralph for a few months. I hung out with Brandon every day. He was like my best friend. He also hated Mr. Ralph and would often tell me he didn't want to be there with him. I never understood why. I was only eight at the time, so I never bothered asking Brandon about his relationship with Mr. Ralph. I just assumed he was his uncle.

Brandon didn't attend school, and I had to sneak and play with him. He would sneak out the back door and wait on my porch until I came out. Brandon never once knocked on the door. Once, he told me his real name wasn't Brandon. I thought he was joking. One day, he was just gone. The only conversation I had with Mr. Ralph over the years was about Brandon.

For some reason, on this day, when I saw Mr. Ralph, I remembered Brandon. I hadn't thought about him in years. I wondered how he looked now. I immediately wondered why Mr. Ralph would lie about Brandon living there and why he suddenly left. He didn't leave a goodbye note or anything. As my thoughts wandered, I looked up, and I was in front of the school building.

I arrived at school right after the bell rang. I didn't like school. I was somewhat popular but only for being

Dawn's twin. The kids also noticed I had style. I wore my navy blue uniform totally different from the other kids. I wore long beige socks and put small cuffs in my pants. My white uniform shirt was perfectly ironed, and I always put on a jean jacket to add some style. My teachers often told me to take it off, but I pretended to be anemic. I bopped down the hallway, moving my head from side to side as if I wore earphones. I stopped at the glass door in the back of Dawn's classroom to peek in. I watched her twirl her hair around her index finger over and over. She looked bored. She slouched in the chair as if she couldn't wait for the class to be over. I watched her eyes keep glancing at a boy named Michael.

All the girls had a thing for Michael. He was one of the taller boys in our grade. He had a caramel complexion, straight Indian-like hair, and an extremely deep dimple. Dawn was now in a deep daydream, and for a moment, I got lost in her mind. I imagined what she was thinking, how she was feeling, or what story she produced in her mind. I had an extreme fascination with Dawn. I felt like we were the same person. I was often curious to know what life was like in Dawn's world. My thoughts were interrupted by the principal.

Mr. Lewis was short and thick, with a huge nose that consumed his entire face. He always wore an oversized suit as if his big brother gave him hand-me-downs. His suit tie always had some stupid character like flamingos or singing ducks. His breath smelled like ass, and he was an underachiever his entire life. The sight of him instantly annoyed me.

"Uhm, Damien, don't you think you have somewhere to be?" Mr. Lewis asked.

"Hi, Mr. Lewis. For sure, I need to be in class. My mother just asked me to give Dawn something," I lied.

"Give it to me, and I'll give it to her. You can get to class because the bell has already rung," Mr. Lewis stated with his hand out, waiting for something I didn't have.

"Well, it was personal. No worries, I can give it to Dawn at lunch," I said, eager to walk away.

"Damien, just hurry up to class," he demanded.

I walked into my classroom late. Everyone looked up and immediately looked back down as if I was a nobody. I could see people look straight through me as if I was invisible. It bothered me to be overlooked. I wanted immediate acknowledgment whenever I walked into a room. The classroom was silent. I stomped over to my seat, slammed my books on the desk, and roughly sat down.

I smirked to myself, as now all eyes were on me. The teacher said something, but I couldn't hear her. I blocked her out. I was too busy enjoying all the eyeballs that stared at me. The school day was long and dreadful. After the bell rang, I was at my locker when I saw Mr. Lewis speed walking towards me with an annoyed facial expression. I instantly slammed the locker and tried to run out the front door. There were too many kids crowded for dismissal. I couldn't maneuver my way through the crowd fast enough.

"Damien!" Mr. Lewis screamed through the hallway.

"Shit," I mumbled under my breath. I reluctantly turned around to see what he wanted.

"You have detention. You were late and disruptive to your class, according to Mrs. Armstrong. Follow me."

"Since when do we get detention for being late? I can't stay after. My Mama expects me home before her to look after Dawn," I lied.

"You are getting detention for being disruptive, not for being late. Why were you late anyway? Dawn is always on time." Mr. Lewis said as he looked at his cheesy watch that sat on his wrist.

"Mr. Lewis, I'm not Dawn. Besides, she's early because she has band practice. Unlike Ms. Perfect Dawn, I have morning chores, and sometimes I lose track of time," I lied again.

"Well, maybe I need to call your mother to discuss all this responsibility you have. School should be the most important thing in your life. You do want a good job one day, right?"

"No, I actually don't. Everyone I know works like a dog, and I have no interest in being an animal."

"That's it! You will learn to control your mouth one day. Detention it is, and it's not up for discussion!" Mr. Lewis said with a raised voice.

There I was, stuck in detention with Mr. Lewis, his stinking breath, his wrinkled-up suit, along with six other students. What kind of principal has no life, so much so that he has time to hold detention after school? Instead of letting the teachers do it. He got some type of weird sensation being in charge of detention.

As I sat in detention, all I could think about was dinner. I was hoping my lousy father didn't show up and ask for extras that Mama would surely give him. It was the extra's my stomach often yearned for after a long day at school. In fact, the later I would be, the smaller my plate would get. If you are not at your seat for dinner at Mama's house, there will be an empty plate at the table, and you will get left with the scraps. My anger lifted from my soul as I thought about Papa eating the last piece of chicken.

"How much longer?" I blurted out.

"Damien, that's why you are in detention in the first place. Did you forget that being disruptive is unacceptable at Dobson Middle?"

"No, of course not, Mr. Lewis," I mocked.

After another dreadful thirty minutes, I was released. I walked home alone in the dark. I cut through the schoolyard football field, and it always seemed scary at night with no people in the stands. It was pitch dark, and all I could see were my long beige socks. I wanted to run, but I knew if I ran, it would feel like someone was chasing me. That frightened me more, so I decided to speed walk, and I never looked back. At some point, I closed my eyes. I slightly opened them as I felt the concrete on the soul of my shoes. I immediately knew I was out of the field and onto the sidewalk back into my neighborhood with the lights. Before I could fully open my eyes, I bumped into Mr. Ralph.

"Hey, young Cat. You need to watch where you going before you stumble in the wrong lap," Mr. Ralph said with a devilish look in his eyes.

"Thanks for the warning. I'll watch my steps next time. Excuse me," I said firmly as I looked away, avoiding eye contact.

"Don't think I don't know who you are. You can fool everyone else, but I know. The question is will I keep it to myself?" Mr. Ralph asked, still blocking me.

"Keep what to yourself?" I asked with my eyebrows raised.

"Oh, you know. I wonder how your parents will feel?"

"Mr. Ralph, I have no idea what you are talking about. But I was thinking about Brandon earlier. What happened to him?" I questioned.

"I done told your little stupid ass, there was never a kid at my house," Mr. Ralph said as he aggressively grabbed my arm.

Get off of my arm!" I screamed so the two thug guys who stood near the corner could turn and look at us.

"Yo, you good?" One guy asked with a look of concern.

"Yeah, I'm good," I responded as I snatched my arm back from Mr. Ralph.

"Yo, is that your kid? Why you grabbing on him like dat?" One guy asked.

"Nah, it ain't nothing, young buck. We were just talking. Right, Damien? Mr. Ralph asked, looking at me for confirmation. I ignored him and walked away.

I was only one block away from my house, and I was starving. I couldn't get Mr. Ralph's comment out of my mind. He said he knew my secret. *How the fuck could he possibly know. Mama didn't even know. He was probably just fucking with me. There's no way he could know.*

I continued to stroll through the neighborhood. I saw papa's car in the driveway, and my stomach instantly felt sick. I opened the metal gate that led to our front door, and I walked in. I heard everyone at the table laughing and joking. I dropped my book bag at the door and made my way to the kitchen. Right when I walked towards my chair, the doorbell rang.

"Get that, Damien, before you sit down," Papa said with a slur in his voice as if he was already drunk.

"No, Jerome, I'll get it. Let the boy eat. Damien, we will talk about why you are late later," Mama said to me as she walked to the door.

"Let's talk about it now! Got damn it," Papa yelled as he belched.

"Jerome, leave it!" Mama yelled to Papa. "Oh, hey, stranger. Jerome didn't tell me you were coming by tonight. I think we have a little dinner left," Mama said to someone at the door.

I quickly dug into my plate. I was so happy I had a piece of chicken on my plate. I wished for another drumstick. I felt Dawn staring at me as I ate like a stray dog. I looked at her, and she smiled and handed me another piece of chicken that was wrapped up in a napkin. I smiled back at her. I never knew what to expect from Dawn. It's like she only loved me sometimes or like she made herself love me. I slammed the fork in the creamy mashed potatoes and immediately went back to eating.

"Hey there, Ralph," Papa said with a fake grin on

his face as Mr. Ralph entered our kitchen.

"I hope my dinner invitation was good for tonight?" Mr. Ralph replied.

I glanced up from my almost empty plate, and I couldn't believe Mr. Ralph was sitting at my dinner table with his pink and brown cow-like lips. I knew he and Papa were friends, but Papa never bought his friends home. Actually, I didn't know much about Papa outside of the house. He was always out getting drunk, and many nights he didn't make it home at all. Mama would stay up all night pacing back and forth like a stupid duck. I started slowly chewing my last bite of food. Panic took over my body. *What if he tells Papa my secret? Papa will surely kill me. What if he lies on me about bumping into him.* My thoughts were rambling, and I fell into a deep daydream.

"Did you hear me, boy? I said, leave the table. It's adults talking now. Do some homework or something," Papa yelled, snapping me out of my thoughts. I gave my plate to Mama and walked towards the stairs.

"Did you hear me, Papa? Leave this house now! It's bills that need to be paid. Pay some bills, make some money, stop being a drunk or do something," I mumbled under my breath as I slowly walked up the steps. I laughed to myself at my witty remarks Papa couldn't hear.

"Why were you late?" Dawn asked soon as I hit the

top step.

"I had detention with Mr. Lewis for nothing. Did you cover for me?" I asked.

"Not this time Damien. I didn't know what to say," she whispered as she walked towards her bedroom.

"Damn it, Dawn. You could have said I had a book club or anything," I said, pacing back and forth. I was nervous because Mr. Ralph could be downstairs exposing my secret, not because of detention, but Dawn didn't need to know that.

"Sit down, stop pacing. Mama may forget all about it, and if she doesn't, just make something up. Watch this show with me and massage my hair," Dawn softly demanded.

"Do I scare you sometimes?" I asked as I rolled my hand up and down Dawn's scalp.

"No. I know you would never hurt me. I do think you lose your marbles sometimes. I always know your heart, so I don't take it personally. Why did you ask me that?" Dawn quizzed.

"No reason. Your hair smells good. Did you rewash it?" I asked as I sniffed harder.

"No, Mama did this time. You like it?"

"Yes, tell Mama to do it like this all the time," I said as I was interrupted by Mama knocking on the bedroom door.

"Damien, I need to talk to you. Dawn, get ready for

bed. Don't think you are going to be up all night watching TV," Mama said as she watched me stand up to meet her in the hallway. My heart raced faster as I heard Mr. Ralph's voice downstairs.

"Mama, whatever he said," I tried to explain before Mama cut me off.

"He, who? Damien, I called you out here to talk because it's something I have to tell you. I can't tell Dawn because she won't be able to handle it," Mama said with her head held low.

"What is it?" I asked with anxiety and fear.

"My job has to let me go, and the bills are already months behind. I may have to split you and Dawn up. You may have to go stay with Aunt Sheryl, and I don't know about Dawn yet," Mama said with a sympathetic tone.

"What? Split us up? Why can't you make Papa pay some bills? Dawn is the only person who loves me," I confessed.

"Dawn loves you very much, and so do Papa and I. Your father does the best he can," Mama lied.

"If the best he can is nothing, then yes, Mama, he does a great job. So, are you only sending me away?" I selfishly asked.

"Papa thought it would be best to let you get adjusted first. You are the boy, and you are the strongest. Dawn will fall apart."

"Of course, Papa thought that. Well, Mama, I'm disappointed. I've tried to be the perfect son, and nothing I do is ever good enough. I'm sorry you lost your job, but I'm also sorry you are sending me away. Good night Mama," I said with no emotion as I hummed to myself, walking down the dark hallway towards my room. I stopped and glanced downstairs, where I saw Mr. Ralph leaving out. He caught eye contact with me and smirked. I gave him an emotionless stare, and I smirked back.

2
YELLOW TAPE

I woke up late, and I had on pajamas. I never wore pajamas. I couldn't remember putting them on. The house was tranquil for a school morning. I didn't hear Mama fussing or Dawn's TV. It was an awkward silence in the house. I sat up from my bed and stretched. I put my foot on the floor, and my toe hit a wood stick with nails. I was grateful I didn't cut myself. I picked up the stick, and I felt confused. I looked at it closer, and it appeared to have specs of dried-up blood.

Everything seemed out of place. I put the stick under my bed as I searched the room. I glanced at the clock on my dresser, which read 9:07 A.M. I was so confused as to why Mama didn't wake me up for school. I walked towards the bathroom to brush my teeth. With my eyes half-closed, I bumped into the side of the wall. I then heard a squeaking sound coming from Mama's room.

"Oh, look who's finally woke," Papa said as he rubbed his linty loose-curled hair. He walked from Mama's room as if he was still asleep himself.

"Morning, Papa. Why didn't Mama wake me up for school?" I questioned.

"Because she's soft. She said you needed a day off to rest and to take in the news she dropped on you last night," Papa said with a smile.

"So that wasn't a dream? You guys are really sending me away?" I asked in a disappointing tone.

"Hell no, it wasn't a dream. Things need to change around here, Boy. I can tell you don't respect me, but that's going to change too," Papa said as he burped a nasty liquor smell.

"Papa, why do you hate me?" I asked in a soft tone.

"Oh, don't play the victim with me, boy. I claim you cause you my blood, but something ain't right with you. I felt it since you were seven years old."

"What could I have possibly done to you at seven years old? Huh? What Papa, what?" I yelled.

"You know damn well what you did. That day I fell in the gutter; I felt someone push me. You weren't close enough to push me, but I know you did it somehow. Then you whispered something into my brother's ear, and he has never been the same. He doesn't even talk anymore. If someone mentions your name, he shakes uncontrollably," Papa yelled, walking closer to me.

"I have no idea what you are talking about. What could a seven-year-old do to a grown man? Uncle Robby was already disturbed, Papa. That's not my fault," I said as I proceeded to walk into the bathroom.

"It was your fault. I can see the evil behind your eyes. You can't fool me. Don't walk away from me, boy," Papa yelled as he grabbed my arm.

"Papa, let me go," I asked in a settled tone.

"Tell me what you did," Papa whispered in my ear as he leaned in.

"If you don't let me go, I will show you what I did to Uncle Robby," I whispered back in Papa's ear.

"I knew it!" Papa screamed as his big solid hand slapped my face. I fell to the floor abruptly. I balled up my fist. Then I slowly released each finger. I stood up with both my hands to my sides as I breathed heavily.

"Papa, you are going to wish you never did that. Excuse me, I need to use the bathroom," I said as I grabbed my composure before walking past Papa.

Papa slowly walked back to the bedroom, staring at me without taking his eyes off me. His stupid ass thought I had some type of powers. I was there the day he fell, and it did look like someone pushed him. It was strange, but it wasn't me. I also didn't make

Uncle Robby's crazy-ass stop talking.

No way was I staying in the house alone with him all day. I got dressed for school, and I didn't care how late I would be. It was disturbing to know Papa set me up to leave my family. On top of that, he wanted to split me up from Dawn. I would indeed have to teach him a lesson—the nerve of that no-good drunk father of mine. I decided I would deal with Papa later but, for now, I had to make my way to school.

I walked outside and felt a cool breeze hit my neck. The air felt heavy, and my senses were off. I couldn't remember a day I woke up without mama and Dawn. The neighborhood was quiet as I walked through the blocks. It almost felt like I was in a dream. I felt my face where papa had slapped me. It was a little sore and slightly bruised. I stopped at the store to get a bag of Doritos since I had skipped breakfast. I opened my chips and crossed the street. I saw a crowd standing around a yellow tape. A woman was crying in a guy's chest.

"What happened?" I asked a nosey neighbor as I took another bite of my Dorito. Her name was Ms. Clara, and she always knew everyone's business.

"Oh child, it's such a tragedy. Someone murdered Ralph last night!" Ms. Clara exclaimed.

"What? Mr. Ralph is dead?" I questioned with no emotion.

"Yes, they say someone beat him to death in his sleep. Who would do such a thing? Ralph never bothered anyone," she whimpered as a tear rolled down her cheek.

"I can't believe that. That's crazy cause Mr. Ralph just had dinner with my father last night," I said with my head hung low as if I was disturbed by the news.

"Dinner? Ralph had dinner at your house last night? Around what time?" Ms. Clara questioned.

"I'm not sure. Maybe I should stay quiet and make my way to school. I don't want to get my Papa in any trouble." I lied.

"Wait! Officer, Officer! Please come here. I think this boy has some information for you," she yelled.

"No, I have to go," I said as I proceeded to walk away.

"Young man, I need to speak with you," The tall, dark detective yelled out to me.

"Yes, Sir," I turned around and answered in an obedient tone.

"Ms. Clara informed us that you saw Ralph Jones last night. Is this true?" the detective asked with a pen and pad in his hand. His eyes looked intense, but excited to be getting a lead.

"I'm not sure if I should say anything, Sir. My Papa won't be happy."

"Well, first, I should introduce myself. My name is

Detective Ross. I'm working on this case. We can bring you down the station with a parent, but we are not questioning you. We just want to know about the last time you saw the victim," Detective Ross stated as he walked away from the crowd.

"Well, I saw Mr. Ralph last night for dinner. He came over unexpectedly, and my father didn't seem too happy about it. My father told me to leave the table so that grown folks could talk, so I went upstairs to watch TV with my twin sister, but she fell asleep. About fifteen minutes later, I heard a loud *BOOM!* Then I heard Papa and Mr. Ralph arguing. Something about some money. Shortly after, I saw Mr. Ralph leave our house upset. That's all I know, officer," I said in a sincere tone.

"That was good. Just a few more questions. Do you know what time the victim, I mean Mr. Ralph left? Do you know if your father left back out?"

"I'm not sure about the time he left; I'm thinking around 10:00. I'm not sure what time Papa left back out. I only heard him stumbling in drunk early this morning. Now can I please go? I'm already super late for school," I pleaded.

"Sure. Thanks for your help. I may have more questions for you later. What's your address?"

"Please don't get me in trouble. Please don't tell my Papa I talked to you," I begged.

"I won't, I promise. Your address, please," the detective demanded with his pen and paper ready to write.

"2219 Brookshire Avenue," I said as I proceeded to walk away.

I walked to school with a big smirk on my face. Although I was late, the school day still seemed to take forever. After the bell rang, I immediately ran to Dawn's class so she could walk home with me. I almost missed her due to Mr. Lewis stopping me to tell me he heard I was late for school again. I just apologized so I could be sure to catch Dawn. I could tell she wanted to walk with her friends, but she saw the look on my face, and she knew to come with me without a fuss.

"Why do you want me to walk with you, Damien? I always go with my friends," Dawn asked in an annoyed tone.

"I have to tell you something. Mr. Ralph was killed last night, and the police pulled me up this morning," I said in an eager tone.

"What? That's so sad. Who would kill him? He was just with us last night. I know Papa will be so sad. That was his friend."

"Did you hear anything last night?" I asked, looking Dawn in the eyes.

"No. Oh my god, that is so sad," Dawn said as she

wiped a tear off her cheek.

"Why are you crying? He wasn't your friend. Well, I told the police he was at our house last night. The police really scared me. I told them you fell asleep so they wouldn't question you. They said Papa and Mr. Ralph had an argument last night. Did you hear anything?" I asked.

"No, you already asked me that, Damien. I don't even know when he left. I fell asleep after Mama called you to the hallway. What did Mama say about you staying after school again?" she asked in a curious tone.

"You know, just the usual. Ok, so if the police question you, just tell them you were asleep. You know I will always protect you, Danny girl. That's all you need to say. Ok?"

"Ok, hopefully, everything will be alright. Poor Mr. Ralph," she whimpered.

We walked across the field. When we hit the concrete, it was awkward not seeing Mr. Ralph standing in his usual spot. He usually sat in a rusty chair by the corner store where he played lottery all day with the other older neighborhood drunks. I didn't miss his slimy face one bit. He made me feel uncomfortable. He disturbed my peace, and I was happy he was gone. I felt nothing for his death except happiness. I was relieved he was gone. Dawn and I walked in the front door and greeted Mama.

"Hi, Babies. I didn't make any dinner tonight. We got some bad news today, and your father is a sad space," Mama expressed with sympathy in her voice.

"What happened, Mama?" I asked in a concerned tone. I felt Dawn giving me the side-eye as we both had already heard the news.

"Mr. Ralph was murdered last night. Try to be nice to your father, that was one of his best friends. He's not taking it so well," Mama explained.

"I'm so sorry, Mama. Damien told me after school. I feel so bad for Mr. Ralph," Dawn said as she sat next to Mama and held her hand.

"I know, Baby. I feel bad for his family. Damien, how did you know?" Mama asked with a serious look.

"I saw the yellow tape on my way late to school. Ms. Clara told me. I was so disturbed walking to school. He was just here last night," I lied.

"I'm sorry you had to hear that way. Clara is always running her damn mouth. Ralph told me last night he wanted to talk to me about you. We were supposed to meet at the store later today. Do you know what he wanted to talk about?"

"I'm not sure. Maybe he wanted to tell you about the basketball program he wanted to start," I lied again.

"Well, I guess, I'll never know. Ralph is gone now,"

Mama wept. Our conversation was interrupted by a loud knock at the door.

I walked to the front door and let the police in as I turned to Mama. It was Detective Ross and his partner. Detective Ross stood tall with his dark ashy skin tone and dark rings under his eyes. He appeared overworked and unflattering. His suit was oversized and wrinkled. His eyes showed a strong determination. You could tell the job was his life, and he took the cases home with him daily. Both detectives started questioning everyone, including me, again.

"Is there anyone else in the house?" Detective Ross asked.

"Just my husband. He's upstairs grieving. He and Ralph were really good friends," Mama explained.

"Good friends, huh? Mr. Jerome, would you mind coming down here so we can have a word with you?" The other detective yelled up to Papa.

"Yeah. What's going on?" Papa asked.

"Did you see Ralph last night? And about what time?" Detective Ross asked.

"Yes, I saw him. He actually came over for dinner unexpectedly. You know we are. I meant we were good friends, but outside of the family. You know what I mean?" Papa stuttered.

"No! What do you mean, Jerome?" The other detective asked.

"I mean, we hung out and had drinks and stuff, but I never been around his family, so I was shocked to see him pop up last night. You know, we were drinking buddies," Papa explained.

"Oh, yeah. I know. At the station, we call those bar pals. Guys you drink with but would never bring home," Detective Ross added with a fake laugh.

"So, the problem is, this was the last place Ralph was seen alive. Did you guys have a fight?" Detective's Ross partner asked.

"Well, Detective, if Ralph died in his bed, we clearly know this wasn't the last place he was alive," Papa shot back.

"Not died in his bed, murdered Mr. Jerome. How did you know he was in his bed? We never disclosed those details," Detective Ross shot back.

"The streets talk. Maybe whoever found Ralph talked about it. Anyway, why all the third degree?" Papa asked Detective Ross with an irritated tone. Ross's partner went to talk to Mama. I stayed there to listen intensely.

"We heard from a little birdy that you guys had a fight last night?" Ross stated.

"Well, your little birdy lied, and now I want you to get the fuck out. Can your little birdy help you with that?" Papa aggressively asked.

"Temper, temper. It would be best if you watched

that. It could get you in trouble. We'll be back. You have yourself a nice day, Mr. Jerome. Thanks, everyone, for your cooperation," Detective Ross stated as he put on his hat and left our house.

"Some fucking nerve, them pussy ass cops coming in here talking that dumb shit. Who the fuck let them in any way?" Papa screamed.

"I did! I just opened the door," I confessed.

"I'm sure you did. I'm not surprised. Baby, can you spare me twenty dollars so I can get a drink? I'll give it back to you Friday," Papa asked Mama.

"Jerome, you don't need a drink. Why do you think they questioned you like that? Did you leave back out last night?" Mama asked.

"Don't tell me what the fuck I need. I just got questioned by the damn cops, and now you are questioning me? I crashed on the couch. I did hear someone leave out, but it wasn't me," Papa said as he looked in my direction.

"Here, just take the money. Go get drunk if you want. I don't care," Mama said as she handed Papa a twenty-dollar bill.

Papa left out and slammed the door. There was an awkward silence in the room. Detective Ross mentioning the little birdy made me nervous. I thought he was going to give me up. Papa not cooperating with the cops didn't look good. It made him look guilty.

Mama told us to go outside for a while. She told us she needed time for herself. Mama was a beautiful woman, but lately, she was letting herself go. She wore her hair in the same ponytail for at least a week. She stood there with her perfectly shaped body saying something, but I couldn't hear her. Papa called her a brick house. I never knew what that meant, but I knew it was a compliment to her body. Mama seemed sad, even before Ralph's death. I think she was tired of being used by Papa.

Papa wasn't always a drunk. He was the slickest dude around, from what we were told. His handsome face caused a lot of female attention. The women flirting with Papa always annoyed Dawn and me. They constantly flirted when Mama wasn't around, but they had no respect for his kids being around. It seemed like the more Papa started to drink, the more he hated me. Only me. He loved Dawn. He thought she was the most perfect thing created. She could do no wrong, and she had him whipped around her fingers.

I went outside, as Mama said, and I found myself lost. It was always hard for me to find my place when I went outside. I couldn't play with the girls, and the boys were dirty, and I hate being dirty. I'm by far the cleanest in the house. I take the most showers, and my appearance matters a lot. I strolled the neighborhood and decided to go to the basketball court. I didn't know how to hoop, but I knew how to pretend.

I bopped extra hard to the basketball court. For some reason, when I had to hang around other boys, I acted harder and tougher. I bopped so hard my knees started hurting. I saw five boys on the court, and I knew one of them from school. I mentally prepared myself to change my entire character. I had to turn into "outside," Damien.

"Yo, can I hoop?" I casually asked.

"Can you play?" One boy asked.

"Yo, y'all going to let me in the game or not? Y'all uneven anyway," I suggested.

"Ard, bet. You can roll with us on this side," One guy agreed.

I knew the basics of the game, so I was able to fake my way through. I mainly bluffed and let the other two do all the work. I was tired after about five minutes. When I finally got the ball, I looked slick shooting it, so it could look like I had a chance of making it in when I missed it. It worked. I did make two shots, and I could barely believe it myself. By the end of the game, I was sweaty and stinky. All the boys were smelly. I wanted to keep hanging out with them but not to play basketball. I guess just to be around other boys.

I was popular enough, but I didn't have many

friends. Dawn was my only real friend, and we were growing apart. I was much different from the other kids. The moment they did something I didn't like, I wanted to kill them. Not just fight them, I wanted them to die. Anyone who hurt me, I wanted to hurt them really bad. It was hard controlling my thoughts. Sometimes, I didn't even know if they were my thoughts.

After two long hours outside, I was relieved to go into the house and shower. When I came home, Dawn had already returned. I walked past her and kicked her hard before running up the steps to go straight to the shower. My showers were an intimate time with myself. I loved getting clean, and I loved jerking off. It's a boy's heaven. Everything is ready for you, soap, water, and privacy.

Two weeks later, I was making a lunchmeat sandwich in the kitchen, and I heard a boom boom at the door. Mama let in the Detroit police department. They had a warrant for Papa's arrest. It was one of the happiest days of my life. My plan had worked. Papa was going to jail. I had successfully framed him.

It wasn't long before they were dragging Papa out of the room. He had his hands behind his back, and he came down the steps kicking and screaming like a two-year-old. I felt so much joy inside, and it was daunting to pretend I was upset. Papa looked angry and confused. I knew Papa being gone wouldn't affect me at all. He didn't pay anything; he didn't cook, and he never helped Mama around the house. Pretty much, it was nothing to miss.

"Let him go. Why are you arresting him?" Mama screamed.

"Ma'am have a seat," the detective told Mama as another officer proceeded to walk Papa out the door.

"Papa, why are they taking you? What happened?" Dawn asked as tears filled her eyes as she ran behind Papa.

"It's okay, Baby, this will all be cleared up," Papa said as the detective walked to the side to converse with another officer. Dawn ran to hug Papa and dropped to her knees. I went on the other side of Dawn and hugged Papa too.

"I guess I won't be the one getting sent away, after all," I whispered loud enough for Papa to hear me. Detective Ross took him out of the house. He screamed devilish remarks about me, and I pretended to cry as I secretly waved bye.

"I don't understand. Why are they arresting him? Why is your father talking about killing you, Damien?" Mama asked.

"Mama, I don't know. You know Papa hates me. He probably said that because I told detective Ross that Mr. Ralph had dinner with us that night," I answered.

"Why the hell would you tell him that?" Mama yelled.

"It's the truth! It's not like I said he killed the man. You wanted me to lie to the police?" I quizzed.

"No, Damien. Did you tell them anything else?" Mama asked in an annoyed tone.

"No! They must have found some evidence or something to lock him up."

"They didn't find shit. They are always ready to lock up a black man. Don't you ever give them a helping hand. The next time the police question you about anything, you tell them you are a child and to call your mother," Mama said with force.

"Are you still making me leave next week? Mama, I don't want to leave. This is my family too," I honestly said.

"I can't talk about that right now. I can't even think," Mama replied.

"Leave? Where is he going?" Dawn finally said something as she continued to cry about Papa.

"I said, not right now!" Mama screamed.

Papa once told me I was evil. Maybe he was right. I didn't feel evil, but I did feel revengeful. I couldn't let anyone get away with anything, and he had to pay for that smack. Getting Papa arrested for murder may seem harsh to some people, but it's the perfect punishment in my eyes. It's better than killing him, which crossed my mind quite frequently. He didn't deserve to be a part of this family. He was a curly head, broke, drunk whore. Mama couldn't see what was best for her. Maybe now, she can be a mother again.

3
TWO OF THE SAME

I stood over Dawn as she peacefully slept. I watched her lips move up and down as she ground her teeth. I admired how much we looked alike. It amazed me how we could have the same face. I often wondered how different my life would've been if I had been the girl. I cared more about my appearance than she did, and it seemed girls had it easier. Well, at least in my house, it felt that way.

I lightly brushed her hair off her face as she snored. I looked behind her ears and observed her ear piercings. I wondered if it hurt her to get a hole punched in her ear. I took my finger and lightly pushed her eyebrow hair back in place. She moved a little, and I didn't budge. She never opened her eyes. I heard my mother stomping up the steps as if she was a four-year-old craving attention. I knew she was still upset that Papa was arrested. I smiled at the thought of Papa rotting away for murder. I made sure to be extra quiet as I heard Mama settle down in her room.

Earlier that night, after Papa was arrested, Mama sent me to Mark's house. Mama was so upset, and I guess the thought of looking at me was disturbing since Papa yelled out all those lies about me. Mark was a younger boy who Mama thought I would want to play with. As if I wanted to play at thirteen years old.

Mark was about ten years old, but he was maturing slowly, or I was too mature at thirteen. Either way, I was too old for sleepovers, but I decided to go along to accomplish my goals. Mark's house would become my alibi. Early that morning, I snuck back into my house just to do what I had been waiting to do forever. Never again will Dawn have something I didn't have. I truly felt twins should be equal.

I patiently waited for Mama to shut her bedroom door. I pulled a pair of black scissors from behind my back and leaned over Dawn's snoring body. I lifted the back of her hair up in the air and performed my first chop. I thought of cleaning up the falling hair, but I reminded myself a stranger wouldn't clean up chopped hair? I was extremely bothered by dirt or clutter. I had the cleanest room in the house, even more, immaculate than Mama's bedroom. I watched the hair fall helplessly to the floor as I continued to chop. I chopped her hair fast and sloppy like Mama chopped her onions for dinner.

I slipped back out the window and returned to Mark's house. I was relieved he was still asleep. I quietly entered Mark's room and felt an instant sense of relief to hear him snoring. I made sure to play the game of who can stay up longer so he would be knocked out for sure when I snuck out. I slowly climbed the ladder that led to his top bunk bed. With each step, I climbed softer and softer. I fluffed the flat pillow that sat on his top bunk and fell asleep.

"What are you doing here?" I thought you died?" I asked Mr. Ralph as I walked closer to him.

"Died? Do you mean murdered? Or did you forget Damien?" Mr. Ralph asked with an evil look on his slimmer-than-usual face.

"Murdered or whatever? Why are you here? I thought I ..."

"You thought you what? Killed me? I will never die until you confess!"

"Confess what? I didn't kill you. I'm glad you are gone, though," I admitted.

"I'm glad you are honest. Now you can be glad to die as well," Mr. Ralph said as he pulled out a gun.

My nightmare was interrupted by yelling from

Mark's mother telling us to wake up. I glanced at the clock and realized I had only got one hour of sleep. Mark's mother was more annoying than Mama in the morning.

"Damien, your mother called upset and asked you to please come home right away," Mark's mother informed me.

"Come home for what? I wanted to hang out with Mark today," I expressed with sadness in my voice. My heart raced as I knew my mother was calling about Dawn's hair.

"I'm not sure, Damien, but wash your face and head home. We can reschedule for another day.

Mark sat silently on the end of his bed with crust in his eyes. I walked home in the clothes I had slept in the night before. Soon as I opened the door, I heard screaming. Not the usual screaming; it was loud and excruciating. I heard streaks of pain every cry. I took great pleasure on the inside.

"Mama! What's wrong? Why is Dawn screaming?" I asked as I shut the front door.

"Damien, get up here NOW!" Mama screamed with force and base.

"Why did I have to leave Mark's house?" I screamed up the steps trying to change the subject as if I didn't know what awaited upstairs.

"Boy! Get your ass up here and stop talking back!"

43

Mama screamed

"I'm here, now what's wrong, Mama?" I entered Dawn's room with no emotion or expression on my face.

"Did you come back home last night?" Mama asked me, looking dead in my face. My heart slightly pounded as fear and anxiety took hold of me. For a split second, I wondered if she saw me last night or maybe she heard me before she shut her bedroom door. I had no choice but to stick to my original plan.

"No, Mama. Why would I come back? I stayed up all night with Mark. Can someone please tell me what's going on?"

"I'm going to call Mark because something just doesn't feel right. Turn around, Dawn, show your brother," Mama said as she grabbed the cordless phone to call Mark's house.

"No. I never want anyone to see me," Dawn cried.

"Danny girl, you can turn around. I'm your twin. We look exactly alike. Whatever it is, I'm sure it's not that bad," I said in a soft tone as I walked towards Dawn.

"It is that bad!" Dawn screamed as she turned to face me.

"What happened? Who the hell chopped your hair like that?" I asked with excitement.

"I don't know! I don't know! I just woke up like

this!" Dawn screamed and cried.

"Did you just curse, boy?" Mama asked me as she held the phone to her ear. "Hello, hi Karen. I'm so sorry for calling so upset this morning. It has been one hell of a day so far. By any chance, did you see Damien leave last night or early this morning?" Mama asked Mark's mother, Karen.

"Really! You think I did this to my twin sister? Wow, I get blamed for everything around here. I guess it's my fault Papa's in prison too?" I yelled in the background.

"Girl, I doubt it if he left out, but to be honest, I did fall asleep around 10:00, and the boys were still up," Karen said to Mama. "Mark, come here!" Karen screamed to call Mark to the phone. "Here, talk to Damien's mom," she said as she handed him the phone.

"Hi, Mark. I just wanted to know what happened last night. Did you and Damien sneak out? What time did you both go to bed?" Mama questioned Mark and looked me directly in my eyes with a look of anger and frustration.

"We had so much fun! We pretended we were on the army base, and we had to guard the base. We watched wrestling and dared each other who could stay up the latest. We stayed up all night, and the sun was almost up. I fell asleep first, and Damien put

Ketchup all over me as punishment for tapping out first. Damien showed me how to take the batteries out of the smoke detector and put them in my walkie-talkies. If we are in trouble, we can put the batteries back," Mark explained in a rambling tone.

"Sounds like you boys had a fun night. So, you sure you and Damien stayed up all night together?" Mama asked in a disappointed tone.

"Yup, for sure. Can he come back over tonight?" Mark asked eagerly.

"Not tonight, but maybe another night. Thanks for your help; tell your mother I'll give her a call later," Mama said as she threw the phone on the bed.

"I hate living here! I can't believe you actually thought I could do something like this," I yelled.

"I'm sorry, Damien. I'm also sorry this happened to you, Dawn. I just can't imagine who would do such a thing. Who would break into our house in the middle of the night and cut Dawn's hair? She never bothers anyone, and who would do such a thing. Everything is going to hell since…." Mama stopped mid-sentence.

"Since what, Mama? Since Papa left?" Dawn whimpered out.

"No, since I lied to Damien. It's time, I confess. Damien, that night in the hallway when I told you I lost my job and you had to leave this summer to make things easier. That was a lie. It's been eating me up. I pray you can forgive me so we can fix our family," Mama confessed with her head hung low.

"You lied about losing your job? Just to get rid of me?" I asked, immediately going into victim mode.

"I never wanted to get rid of you, Damien. Papa just expressed some concerns, and he wanted to see how the house would feel without you before we went to get you some help. Papa had those horrible nightmares, and you were always in them. I think it made him a little crazy. He started thinking you were possessed, and he was completely convinced you did something to Uncle Robby. I told him time after time; it was no way you could've made Uncle Robby go insane. I'm so sorry, Damien; I just didn't talk to you about this. It's a weird topic, you know?" Mama asked.

"No, I don't know, Mama. How could it possibly be my fault Papa was having nightmares? What kind of help do you think I need? I have good grades, not as good as Dawn, but they are pretty good. I do all my chores, have the neatest room in the house, keep myself well-groomed, and never ask for anything. What would possibly make you think I needed mental help?" I said in a disturbed tone.

"I don't know, Damien. Papa was convinced. He talked about it so much, and maybe I started believing it. You are an overall good boy. Sometimes just strange things happen in your presence. I can't quite put my finger on it. Anyway, we are family, and we are all we got. I'm sorry for doubting you or even considering splitting you and Dawn up. Do you forgive me?" Mama asked as she reached her hand out for consolement.

"Dawn, I'll help you do something with your hair. Stop crying. You know when you cry, my heart hurts too," I told Dawn, completely ignoring Mama.

I slowly walked out of the room and glanced at Mama as her head hung low. I felt nothing for Mama. She better be lucky I didn't chop off her little bit of hair. How dare she try to throw me away. If I weren't so tired from staying up last night, I would find something to do to her ass right now. She better wake up and make me some fucking biscuits. As for Dawn, oh how I love my Danny girl. I'm sorry she had to pay the price with her hair, but she shouldn't have anything more than me. We are one. We are two of the same.

I walked to my room in silence. I tried to dig deep and find any sense of remorse for butchering Dawn's hair. Not only did I feel nothing, but it also became funny. I found myself laughing out loud in an obnoxious haunted laugh. The more I laughed, the better I felt. I laughed louder and louder.

I heard someone walk down the hallway and stand

at my door. They listened, and I hoped it wasn't Dawn. I would never want her to think I would tease her at a time like this. I kept laughing as I slowly walked to the door. Instead of asking who was there, I snatched the door open quickly. Mama tilted into my room as she almost fell from having her ear so close to the door.

"May I help you, Mama?" I calmly asked.

"No, I was just walking by and stopped to make sure you were okay? Mama lied while avoiding eye contact.

"Mama, I know you heard me laughing. Don't believe what Papa told you. I'm not possessed. You don't have to be afraid of me."

"Why were you laughing like that?" Mama finally asked.

"Mama, I don't want to talk about it anymore. I can't forget that fast that you lied just to get rid of me. For tonight, I'm just going to bed. See you for breakfast," I said as I softly shut the door in Mama's face.

4
A MOTHER'S LOVE

"How come you won't die? You skinny sack of shit!" I yelled to Mr. Ralph. His face was half gone, as if his body was rotting away.

"Confess, boy! Maybe you can have a decent life. I will never go away until you tell the truth!" Mr. Ralph said as he walked towards me with a knife.

"Why are you here. You should be happy your worthless life is over. All you did was drink," I said as I walked on a purple ground.

"You should be nicer to me. I still know your secret, and now you have two secrets since I'm rotting away under the concrete," Mr. Ralph laughed uncontrollably.

"Leave! Leave! Leave!" I screamed as I tossed and turned.

I woke up in a sweat. My clothes were drenched, and my head felt hot. I sat up on my bed and removed my shirt. My nightmares were getting worse. I sniffed the air and smelled homemade buttermilk biscuits just as I wanted. Mama knows she better do what I say.

"Damien! Get up! Mama is making buttermilk biscuits. Hurry up downstairs," Dawn yelled in my room as she happily skipped down the steps two at a time.

"It smells so good in here," I said as I walked into the kitchen.

"Thanks, Damien. Glad to see you are talking to me again. I don't know what came over me. I had this strong urge to make buttermilk biscuits, and I know they are both of you all's favorite," Mama said as she grabbed the oven mitt. Her apron was covered in flour, and she had made three pans of biscuits.

"We are family, right? That's what you said. I still don't like you and Papa's theories about me, but for now, we are family," I said as I glanced at Dawn, who looked ridiculous with her chopped-up hair. She tried to gel it to the side. It was an awful sight. I snickered under my breath as I grabbed the butter and dug in.

I was sitting in the living room after breakfast. Whenever Papa called from jail, I either hung up on him or answered just to annoy him. Dawn worshipped the ground Papa walked on, and so did Mama. I heard the phone ring, so I grabbed the phone near the dining room and dragged the phone with the long cord back to the sofa.

"Hello!" I answered.

"You have a collect call from, "Jerome Scott," If you would like to accept this call, press one," the operator spoke on the other line.

"Hello, hello. Whoever picked up the phone can hang up now. I got it," Mama yelled down the steps as she pressed one. I pretended to hang the phone up as I kicked back my feet, anticipating hearing what Papa had to say.

"Hello. Hey Baby. I miss you so much. Guess what?" Papa asked Mama.

"What? I hope it's good news," Mama said with stress in her voice.

"The shakes stopped. I think all the alcohol is out of my system. Have you talked to the lawyer this week?"

"Oh, Baby, that's great news. I hope you never pick up that bottle again. The lawyer said he needs $200 more before he will represent you. I don't know where it's going to come from. I already emptied my savings," Mama confessed.

"I'm sorry this has happened to us. Did you try to talk to that thing living in our house? Did I tell you the nightmares stopped since I've been away from him?"

"Jerome, he's not a thing. He is our son! I did speak with him, and his story is consistent. He said he would never get you arrested. Why would the cops believe a kid anyway?"

"I don't know why! That little son of a.." Papa screamed before mama cut him off.

"Calm down, now. He's our son. I wanted to tell you something, but you already seem upset, so never mind."

"No, tell me. I'm calm now. Sorry about that. It's just, I'm rotting away in jail for something I didn't do. I can't control my temper sometimes."

"Well, strange things have been happening. Someone cut off all Dawn's hair in the middle of the night, and I felt possessed this morning. I felt as if someone made me get up at the crack of dawn and make biscuits. I can't explain it."

"It's that boy! Get him out of there! You know damn well who cut her hair. My precious baby girl. Is she okay? What if he kills her? Or you? His rage is growing, Sandy. Do something!" Papa demanded.

"Hello, Hello. Jerome, are you still there?" Mama screamed in the phone.

"Mama! Is everything okay?" I yelled upstairs as I held a pair of Mama's garden scissors behind my back.

"No, the phone just died while I was talking to Papa. Did you hear anything?"

"No, Mama. I'm just sitting on the sofa watching TV. Dawn is outside with her stupid friends," I said as I put the scissors back in the kitchen drawer.

"Maybe something is going on with the phone lines. I'm sure it will be fixed soon. I'm a little tired, Damien. I woke up so early this morning, I'm taking a nap. Listen out for your sister," Mama said as she shut her bedroom door.

Papa still didn't learn his lesson. I heard him tell Mama to do something about me. That's precisely why I cut the phone line. Mama said she was napping, but I could hear her fumbling around in her room. I glanced at the hallway mirror that stood close to our steps and noticed my hair looked rough. I despised looking thrown together. I grabbed my brush from my back pocket and hummed as I brushed my hair for at least 15 minutes until I felt every piece of hair was in place. I threw the brush next to a family picture that sat on a table under the mirror. I slowly walked up the steps humming.

I quietly cracked open Mama's door and what I saw was unbelievable. Mama was under the bed with her two hands together. She prayed in a weird chanting tone. Her words sounded like gibberish, and for once, I was actually concerned. I just quietly shut the bedroom door. I hummed as I slowly went down the steps.

I grabbed my brush and went to the window. I saw Dawn sitting with her best friend, Brianna. I didn't like how close they were, and maybe it was time I did something about it. I watched Dawn tell Brianna what to do. Dawn was quiet, but she also had a bossy side that no one rarely saw. Brianna and Dawn were night and day. I never knew what they had in common. I envied the friendship they shared. My only real friend Brandon or whatever his real name was, had disappeared years ago.

Thirteen is such an awkward age. I was maturing fast. I had urges to have sex, and being a kid was becoming less fun every day. I talked to Dawn about sex, and she thought it was disgusting. She also expressed her hate for gay men. I questioned why she would hate someone's sexual preference, and she said the traditional cliché bullshit. "Men should be with women." I had hoped to have the kind of relationship with Papa to talk about sex, but that would never happen. My thoughts were interrupted by Dawn slamming the front door.

"Damien, why were you watching us from the window like a creep? That was embarrassing," Dawn asked, looking at me with a look of disgust as she took her shoes off.

"A creep? I was just thinking about fucking your best friend," I lied.

"Damien, leave her alone. Don't mess with Brianna. She doesn't deserve to get caught up in whatever you have going on in that sick mind of yours."

"Look at you talking trash. Not little Ms. Dawn. Not the girl who does nothing. Why do you want to fuck her?"

"Yuck. Damien, you know I hate that gay stuff. It's a sin. Papa said all people like that will burn forever," Dawn expressed with judgment.

"Burn forever? Papa is always talking about something being a sin. He's never been to church a day in his life. Forget about Papa. What do you think?" I asked while opening a can of soda.

"I think it's against humanity! I agree with Papa. It makes me feel weird. Don't ever say things like that to me again," Dawn demanded as she sneakily rolled her eyes.

"I think how people live is none of you or Papa's business, and Papa shouldn't be judging anyway the way he fucks everyone in the neighborhood. Isn't that a sin too?" I asked.

"Okay, Damien. I'm not about to play these games with you. Papa flirts a lot, but he doesn't sleep with those women. Please just leave Brianna alone," Dawn said, walking towards the steps.

"I'll leave her alone after I fuck her," I mumbled

under my breath.

Once the urge to break up Dawn's friendship with Brianna inserted into my mind, there was nothing I wouldn't do to accomplish my goal. I had this weird obsession with Dawn, I wanted her all to myself, but I couldn't stand her. I envied her. She was everything I wasn't, but she belonged to me. She couldn't deny me, and she couldn't choose to hate me. It would be like hating herself.

Mama said we were unique twins, and the doctors had never seen anything like it. The entire pregnancy only showed one baby, not two. Every sonogram, heartbeat, and lab work only showed one fetus. When Mama pushed us out, Dawn came out first, and the doctor announced, "It's a beautiful girl!" The nurses informed Mama she would have to push again for the afterbirth. She pushed, and I came out. They announced, "Oh wow, it's another baby."

There I lay cold, crying, and unwanted. Mama already had her beautiful baby girl in her arms, and it took an effort to pick up another baby. Mama said she was confused as they laid me in her other arm. She looked down at two strangely identical twins. She couldn't tell who was the girl or who was the boy. I had a mole on my face which helped her tell us apart. Mama always fussed about how Papa was late and how he missed our birth.

Papa entered the hospital room and was shocked to see Mama holding two babies. He asked, "Which one was born first? That's the one I will hold first." He grabbed Dawn and fell in love. He never reached back to pick up the other baby, which was the beginning of our disconnected toxic relationship. That was the beginning of me being an outcast. Everything was pink, and nothing was blue.

Dawn's name was thoughtfully picked out months before her arrival. Mama noticed one of the nurse's name was Damien, and they named me after him. The best part of Mama's story is the ending. She said although Papa only held Dawn when he sat next to me, Dawn reached her little one-day arm out for me. Mama pulled us closer, and we locked hands. Dawn is the only one who has cared for me since day one and I can't allow anyone to take that away from me. So, I must end her friendship with Brianna; they are too close. When I was in the window watching them, I saw Dawn reach her arm out for her. Watching Dawn reach for someone else's hand triggered intense jealousy inside of me. It would be their downfall.

5
A CRUSH

"Please don't. Stop! Don't do this," I screamed as Mr. Ralph stood over top of me with a wooden stick with nails.

"Don't do what, Damien? Don't butcher you, like you did me? Does my face look pretty, Damien? Look at my deep scars?" Mr. Ralph asked as he lifted his hand to swing the stick at my face.

"No, please. I don't even remember killing you," I blurted as I tossed and turned.

"How convenient for you to forget what you did to me?"

"Didn't you forget what you did to Brandon? Please let me up!"

"Let you up? Did you let me up when I was screaming? I didn't do anything to that boy."

"You did! What was his name? Can you tell me that before you kill me?" I asked Mr. Ralph with fear in my eyes.

"Damien! Damien! Damien!" Mr. Ralph screamed.

"Damien! Boy, do you hear me?" Mama yelled, waking me up from my daunting nightmare.

"I'm up, Mama. I'm coming," I yelled as I sat up, wiping the sweat off my forehead. I was so happy Mama woke me up. These nightmares were really starting to piss me off.

"Did you say something about killing?" Mama asked with her eyebrows raised.

"No, Mama. Why do I have to go visit Papa? You know he hates me."

"He doesn't hate you, Damien. We are all going as a family, so get dressed. I'm back in control now. I'm not sure what's been happening around here lately, but it stops today.

"What do you mean, Mama?" I asked with a puzzled facial expression as I stretched.

"I mean all this freaky weird shit that's been happening. Me acting scared in my own damn house. And you running around here laughing like a fucking psycho ain't helping. People chopping off Dawn's hair and shit," Mama expressed as she brushed her hair in my doorway.

"Mama sounds like regular family crap to me," I laughed as I stood up to go to the bathroom.

"Well, this ain't no damn lifetime movie. After you get dressed, go get Dawn from Brianna's house,"

Mama said before shutting my door.

I got dressed and walked to Brianna's house. Brianna lived in a ranch-style house a few blocks away from us. Her place was nice and modern, unlike our old, outdated house. The only thing that I didn't like about their home was there were no steps. Everything was on one level. I knocked on the door, and no one answered. I walked to the side of the house, where I peeked in the window and saw Dawn and Brianna dancing together in her stand-up mirrors.

Brianna's room was disgustingly pink, which I thought was immature for a middle schooler. She was an only child, so it seemed like she had every possible thing a girl would want. Now I understood why Dawn liked being there so much. They had the music blasting as they danced and laughed. I observed Brianna, who was taller. She was fair-skinned, with brown freckles surrounding her nose. She was well developed and had the body of a grown woman, unlike Dawn's flat chest boy body. Brianna looked much older than her age, and it often made her look awkward and out of place. I went back to knock on the front door, but this time louder.

"Oh, hey, Damien. The girls are in the back, doing lord knows what. You can go get your sister," Brianna's mom said as she opened the door in a robe with her oversized breast peeking out. Something about her annoyed me. I don't know if it was her big breast or the fact that she always came to the door half-dressed.

"Thanks. It smells good in here," I complimented as I walked towards Brianna's room.

"Thanks, Damien. I'm just cooking a little something."

I entered the bedroom, and Dawn's face looked annoyed, and she seemed shocked to see me there. Brianna looked at me and smiled. I knew she had a crush on me, but she was annoying. I decided maybe it was time I pursued her more; that way, I could easily accomplish my goal. I looked around her room. I picked up her pink jewelry box and looked inside.

"Put her stuff down, Damien. Why are you here?" Dawn rudely asked.

"Don't tell me what to do. I'm here to see Brianna, not you!" I stated as I threw the jewelry box back on Brianna's pink desk.

"You are here to see me?" Brianna asked with a confused but flirty look on her face.

"Yeah, I want you to meet me later. I'll give you the details when someone is not around," I said as I looked towards Dawn.

"She will be busy later," Dawn loudly stated.

"Girl, no, I won't. We can meet Damien," Brianna said with a smile.

"Cool. I will knock on your window when I'm ready. Dawn, Mama, said come home now. We have to go visit your jailbird, Papa," I laughed as I walked out of Brianna's room. I decided to wait outside her bedroom door.

"You are so lucky you are an only child. Brianna, please don't meet with Damien. You are my friend, and that's my brother," Dawn said in an annoyed tone.

"Girl, you know how long I had a crush on Damien. We will always be friends, but I have to take my chance. Plus, we don't even know what he wants," Brianna stated naively.

"You don't know him, and you have no idea what he's capable of. Just please stay away. Pretend you are asleep when he comes to the window later. Please, Brianna," Dawn whispered in a begging tone.

"You are tripping. You are acting like Damien is a serial killer or something. Everything will be fine. Now go before your mother gets mad," Brianna pushed Dawn out of her room with laughter.

"What am I capable of?" I scared Dawn as she came out of the room.

"Nothing Damien. I just don't want you talking to my friends," Dawn expressed. She seemed shocked I was still in the house, and her eyes seemed fearful.

"Why do you look so scared, Danny girl? Maybe you should watch your mouth and take your own advice. Like you said, "You have no idea what I'm capable of," I opened Brianna's front door and gestured for Dawn to walk out first.

Mama sat on the sofa when we arrived at the house, looking annoyed. Instead of fussing about how long we took, she just told us to hurry up in the car. We had to get to some bus station and catch a bus to see Papa. I was confused on why Mama couldn't just drive to the jail, but I didn't ask any questions. We arrived at the bus just in time to get on. The bus was crowded with multiple families, crying babies, grandmothers, and all kinds of different groups of people.

There were two open seats in the front and one single seat in the back. Mama told me to sit in the back, and it was a two-hour ride so just try to get some sleep. I sat next to an older man who favored Mr. Ralph. That was the last place I wanted to sit, but we were late, and there was only one other seat open next to a lady and her crying baby. I decided to sit next to Mr. Ralph look-alike. The bus was noisy. I took my jacket off and used it as a pillow against the bus window, and it wasn't long before I was asleep.

"You have some nerve going to see my friend after what you did to me," Mr. Ralph whispered in my ear as he sat in the seat next to me.

"How did you get here? Why do you keep bothering me?"

"You knew it was me when you sat down. Am I bothering you? You thought you could just kill me, and I would go away?" Mr. Ralph asked with a grin.

"What do you want? It's not like I can bring you back. What do you want?" I asked more aggressively.

"I want my life back, you little piece of shit. Oh, and you better leave that little girl alone. I mean it! You think I'm haunting you now. You just wait," Mr. Ralph said with a knife in his hand.

"The nerve of you to tell me to leave a little girl alone, should I leave her alone, the way you left the other little girls alone," I asked.

"Give me what I want, Damien!" Mr. Ralph said as he put the knife to my neck.

"What do you want? What do you want? What do you want? I hate you!" I screamed.

The older man sitting next to me woke me up with a shake. I jumped back. I thought he was Mr. Ralph. My nightmares were getting out of control. I know I hated Mr. Ralph, and I wanted him dead. I know I framed Papa for his murder, but I couldn't remember actually killing him. I thought maybe I blacked out. I had a lot of blackouts when I was younger. I would do things that I couldn't remember. Dawn helped me a lot. She always told me what happened during my blackout. I needed the nightmares to stop. I was constantly exhausted, and I started to fear sleep. Even with the nightmares, I still thought Mr. Ralph deserved to be dead. I didn't just want Mr. Ralph dead because he knew my secret; it was more than that. He didn't know I knew one of his secrets too.

One day, I cut school after lunch. I came home and decided I wanted the house to myself. Mama was still at work, and Dawn came in from school later that day. I heard Dawn coming up the porch steps, and I ran to the hallway closet. I looked through the lines in the closet door. I watched her drop her book bag and go straight to the fridge. Something about watching people when they were unaware was so exciting.

I watched her pick boogers from her nose and pluck them on the floor. She was so disgusting. Then someone knocked on the door. She yelled, "Damien," assuming it was me coming in from school, but it wasn't me. It was Mr. Ralph. He told her he was meeting Papa there, but he picked her up an Ice cream. He asked where I was? Dawn told him I would be home from school soon.

They sat on the couch and what happened next freaked me out. Mr. Ralph put his slim wrinkled hands up Dawn's skirt. Dawn nervously jumped. He told her to calm down as he slowly licked her ice cream. Mr. Ralph continued to keep his hand up Dawn's skirt as Dawn uncomfortably sat there. I was furious. I didn't understand why Dawn allowed him to do that. I wondered if it was his first time messing with her. I looked into Dawn's eyes, and I could tell she didn't like it. I could tell she was fearful.

Dawn finally decided to get up. He pulled her back down. He told her it was a sin to wear such a short skirt around men. The nerve of these hypocritical drunks telling someone what's a sin. I continuously stared at the bat that sat in the closet next to the mop and broom. I had to turn away. I couldn't watch Mr. Ralph hurt Dawn. I peeked enough times to make sure he didn't go further than fondling, as if that wasn't enough. Right as I grabbed the courage to grab the bat, Dawn tried to move away again. She told him I would be home soon and he should leave. Mr. Ralph smiled and said, "Oh, Damien is a sinner too." He then released Dawn's arm, and she stood up and pulled her skirt down.

For the life of me, I couldn't understand why Dawn was so weak. Why did she let people do whatever they wanted to her? I was upset with myself for sitting in the closet watching. I regretted not helping her. Although I sometimes did evil shit to Dawn, I never wanted anyone else to hurt her. From that day forward, I grew strong hate for Mr. Ralph, and I wanted him dead. I imagined killing him and what it would feel like. I went over the different ways I could kill him. I despised the sight of him. But with all that, I still can't remember killing him. I've thought long and hard, and I can't replay the act in my mind.

"Last stop, Beacon Penitentiary," the bus driver yelled. It instantly snapped me out of my daydream.

6
HE'S STILL MY PAPA

We entered the jail, and the process was horrific. I already didn't want to see Papa, and then we had to take a two-hour ride. Not to mention we had to pretty much strip down to nothing just to see him. I was beyond irritated. I also started feeling bad for putting Papa in such a horrific place. Yeah, he was a drunk who hated me, yeah, he cheated on Mama and never paid any bills, but he was still my Papa. There's no limit to what I will do when I'm angry. My emotions are uncontrollable, but I feel they are justifiable. I think my actions equal the emotions I display. Maybe I made a mistake putting Papa in this filthy place, or maybe not.

I could never say it wasn't him that committed the murder because it could imply it was me. I was a little nervous about seeing Papa. Everyone thinks I'm so evil, but I do have a compassionate side. I just don't know how to deal with my pain. My pain feels so heavy inside of my gut; it screams to get out. I have to let someone endure my pain. It's my only freedom. Evil, I'm not. Hurt I am. I felt a lack of love since my birth, and since then, something empty has entered my soul. It has no place. It's just there. I'm always starving for affection and attention, and I never get it. I watch Mama give Papa affection, and I watch Papa give Dawn attention, and I watch Dawn force herself to give me attention.

I am the black sheep of this family. I am the one no one wants to deal with. I'm the most unloved. I willingly accept my role, but it never stops feeling bad. I constantly yearn to be the favorite. I always want to take Dawn's place, and that will never change. I will never give this family more than they deserve. It doesn't stop me from loving them. I'm forced to love. It's truly a thin line between love and hate. I am love, and I am hate. The same way I am my father's blood. He can reject me, but it won't change the fact that I'm his seed. I was watered and cared for in Mama's womb, and I will be forever connected to them both.

"Hey, Papa! I've missed you so much," Dawn

yelled as she walked towards Papa, who sat at a white table in the visitor's area.

"Hey, Baby Girl. I couldn't wait to see your precious face. How are you doing, Damien?" Papa asked as he looked me in the eyes. I turned away.

"I'm fine, Papa. How are you?" I finally looked at Papa, whose eyes looked solid and sober. Papa was a handsome man, and I had hardly ever noticed how nice his eyes were because he always had a drunk look. His skin was clear, and he even had muscles. His appearance shocked me.

"Well, to be honest, I could be doing better if I was home with you all. Hello, my gorgeous wife, it's so good to see you. This has really made my day," Papa said to Mama with a smile.

"I can't believe how buff you are. You really look good, Jerome. Well, kids, me and Papa need to talk to you about something, and we want you to be honest," Mama said in a nervous tone.

"I know I haven't always been there for you guys. I know I made a lot of mistakes, and I broke your trust. Damien, we've had a rocky relationship, and that's mostly my fault. You just wanted the best for your mother, and I wasn't always the best candidate. I know why you had me arrested. You were upset because I smacked you, and I understand. But now this is serious. I am being charged with murder. They are about to move me to a high-security prison, and I need you to tell the truth before my trial," Papa pleaded, looking at me.

"Papa, you think it's my fault you are in here?" I asked with a confused look.

"I'm not pointing fingers, Damien, but we all know what you told the detectives. Speaking of that, me and Mama have a few questions about that night," Papa said, looking at Mama

"Can I go to the vending machine? Mama, I'm starving after that long bus ride," Dawn asked as she stood to get money from Mama.

"Just wait, Dawn," Mama snapped. We need to ask everyone who lives in the house this question," Mama stated, motioning Dawn to sit back down.

"The night Ralph died, I was on the sofa intoxicated. I heard the front door shut. I was too tipsy to move, but someone left out of the house that night. Who was it?" Papa asked.

"Not me, Papa!" Dawn instantly yelled out.

"I didn't leave either," I quickly responded after Dawn.

"Well, someone left out. I'm sure of it. I may have been a drunk, but my ears work better than a mouse. You can tell the truth. I just want to know where you went," Papa said, looking towards me.

"Oh, let me guess, you all think I did something to

Mr. Ralph? What kind of evil creature do you think I am? You honestly think I'm capable of murder? That's why I didn't want to come here. Everything is always Damien's fault," I said as I turned my head, looking towards the exit door.

"We know you wouldn't murder someone Damien, they are just asking," Dawn said with sympathy in her eyes.

"Okay, everyone, calm down. We brought you here because strange things have been happening in the house. I think it's time we speak to someone for everyone's safety. I spoke to a lady who will help us. She's coming to the house next week," Mama said.

"Can we go?" I rudely asked.

"Before you all leave, please know I love you. Damien, please think about speaking to the police. We can still fix this," Papa pleaded.

We stopped at the vending machine for Dawn, and we left the visitor's room in silence. I couldn't believe the visit was a bombard to set me up. Mama was bold enough to tell me her plans a week in advance. If she thinks I'm leaving this house quietly, she has sadly underestimated my strength. She's such a fucking liar.

As for Papa, it's either him or me, so I'm not telling the detectives shit. What really has me puzzled is how weird Dawn was acting. I know her well, and she was off. Maybe she couldn't handle seeing her precious

Papa in jail, or perhaps she was lying about something. I'll figure it out later; for now, I have to focus on putting Mama in her place and finishing up with Brianna. Dawn makes me sick; she's always acting like the perfect child. She tried to be nice to me at Papa's visit, but I didn't forget her telling Brianna to stay away from me like I'm an animal.

We took the long two-hour ride home without talking to each other. I sat next to a lovely older lady who gave me a piece of butterscotch candy. Mama and Dawn sat in front of us in silence. The lady told me I favored her grandson. She was the kindest person I had encountered in such a long time. I wanted to hug her or lay on her arm. It was so weird because I almost whispered to her that my family was trying to kill me and could she please take me to live with her. I decided to stay quiet. I thought about the possibility of her calling the police, then I would be stuck in foster care. I glanced at the clock in the front of the bus, which read 8:16 p.m.

I started recognizing street signs, so I knew we were close to Mama's car. I just had to figure out how I could sneak out of the house to get to Brianna's window. We finally arrived home after Mama stopped at a fast-food restaurant to get us a quick dinner. Mama despised fast food. She felt a woman should cook for her family. She complained the entire time about how filled with junk the food was. I glanced at our living room clock, which read 9:19 P.M. I excused myself from the table.

"Mama, I'm about to shower and get ready for bed," I told Mama.

"Ok, Damien. Hurry up because I'm exhausted as well. I'm bathing and going straight to sleep," Mama replied.

"Mama, you can go first. I know you are tired," I suggested.

"Yes, it's been a long day. Tomorrow, let's talk. Tonight, let's just get some rest," Mama replied.

"Mama, can I stay at Brianna's house tonight?" Dawn asked while spitefully looking at me.

"Not tonight. Maybe next weekend."

"But we had plans, Mama. I asked you a week ago, and you said yes."

"No buts Dawn. I don't remember, and it's too late to be going to someone's house."

Mama was asleep in 45 minutes. I found Brianna's phone number in Mama's black book. I prayed Brianna would answer instead of her slutty mother. She answered on the first ring. I told her to pick a fight with Dawn so she wouldn't follow me to her house. Dawn was refusing to go to sleep. She watched my every move. I heard Dawn's room phone rang, and I patiently listened.

"Hello! Hey Brianna girl," Dawn answered excitedly

"Hi, Dawn. I was thinking I need a break from you. I'm always there for you, and you come to my house just to boss me around, and I'm sick of it," Brianna sternly stated.

"What? Stop playing Bri. I tried to get my mother to let me spend the night, but she said no. Girl, I have so much to tell you about the visit to see Papa."

"I don't want to hear about the visit. Are you deaf? I don't want to deal with you anymore. I'm not playing. Stay away from me. Maybe we can be friends at another time, but for now, I need a break!"

"Are you serious? We've been friends since the 4th grade, and now you need a break?" Dawn asked in a sad tone.

"No, Dawn! You've been bossing me around since the 4th grade, and now I'm tired. You never ask whether you can come to my house. You just show up and do whatever you want in my room. You even take my stuff home without asking me."

"Okay. I have been a little bossy, but it's just because everyone bosses me around in my house. I'm sorry. I promise to treat you better," Dawn pleaded.

"Too late. Just give me some time to myself. Please!" Brianna stated harshly before she hung up in Dawn's ear.

I heard Dawn pacing back and forth, and I knew Brianna did as I told her. I heard Dawn whispering in a weird tone to herself. She mumbled random words to herself. I knew she was upset, but it was her fault. If she would've left me alone to see Brianna, she wouldn't be in that position. Now all I had to do was knock on Brianna's window and get her to come with me. I briefly thought about standing her up because she hurt Dawn enough, which was the mission. I wanted Dawn to myself and that best friend shit needed to come to an end.

For some reason, I felt the need to follow through with my original plan. I knew for sure it would end their friendship forever. I felt terrible for Dawn, but I knew what was best for her. She was confused, and she didn't understand that all she needed was me. We started in the womb together. We didn't even need Mama and Papa, but she couldn't see it. As some time passed by, I no longer heard Dawn's cries. I quietly peeked my head in her room, and she appeared to be asleep.

I grabbed my backpack, put my keys around my neck, and slowly walked down each creaking step. I constantly looked behind me. The house was pitch dark, and I couldn't see if Dawn was watching me or not. I saw a man figure at the bottom of the steps who reminded me of Mr. Ralph. I wasn't sure if it was a shadow or if Mr. Ralph figured out how to haunt me while I was awake. I thought of turning around and going back to my room and dismissing the entire plan. Something in my gut told me to leave Brianna alone, but the shadow was gone when I turned back around, so I walked out the front door. When I shut the front door, I knew something inside me would change forever.

7
GONE

I arrived at Brianna's window, and I saw her pacing back and forth. I lightly tapped the window. Her face glowed with excitement when she saw me there. I could tell she had been waiting, but her face didn't look annoyed. She was smiling from ear to ear. I knew at that moment I was an evil person. Perhaps Papa was right. Maybe I didn't deserve to be part of our family.

How could I do a malicious act on an innocent girl? My actions were always justifiable, but this time I had no explanation of why I was involving Brianna. Her smile was captured in my mind like a picture frame. I didn't know at the time, but I would never forget the smile on her face. I contemplated my actions and decided Brianna would have to, unfortunately, endure some of my pain.

"What took so long? I've been waiting all day. I didn't even go to dinner with my family because I was afraid I would miss you." Brianna admitted with a smirk.

"Sorry, the jail bus took forever, and then your best friend was acting like a stalker," I laughed.

"She has been acting so weird. She always tells me to stay away from you and stuff like that. She never says why. Well, I took care of her for the night. I hope she will forgive me in the morning. I would hate to be on her bad side," Brianna said with her head down.

"Yeah, she will. You are her only friend. That's enough about my sister. Are you coming out or not."

"No! Come in here. My parents never come into my room, and they never wake up once they are asleep. They have lots of sex, and I don't see them until the morning. They are actually pretty disgusting," Brianna stated with a look of disgust.

"Girl, I'm not coming in there. It would be just my luck. Come out, we can just go to the field. It's hot out, and I have water and stuff in my backpack. What are you scared?" I asked with my hand reached out.

"Boy! Scared of what? Don't underestimate me," she said as she grabbed my hand and jumped out her window. She closed the window and stood behind me.

"So why did you want me to come so bad?" I asked as we started crossing the street.

"Damien, I know you knew I had a crush on you since forever. You never seemed to pay me any attention. I knew this day would come one day," she said with a sexy smile.

"Is that why you always stared at me? I thought you were a little slow or something," I laughed.

"Real funny!" Brianna punched my arm. "So what are we going to do on the field?" she asked with a curious face.

"I'm a give you what you want."

"And, what do I want?"

"You said you are a big girl now. Let's see!" I said as I licked my lips. We arrived on the field, and I pulled out some of Papa's old liquor and a blanket.

"It's so dark out here. I've never been out here at night. It's kind of creepy but romantic."

"Yes, it's pitch dark. I've been a little scared walking through here alone at night. I had to come this way a few times when I had detention. But you can relax. Here take a drink," I handed her the bottle of Seagram's gin.

"No, thank you. I hate alcohol. I tried it once, and it's disgusting," Brianna said as she pushed the bottle back.

"Yeah, me too. My father made me hate it. Take off your shirt," I demanded.

"Straight to the point, huh. Honestly, Damien, I'm

a little nervous. I'm still a virgin," she paused. "But I want to lose my virginity to you," Brianna whispered.

"Don't be nervous. I'm a virgin too," I admitted as I unsnapped her bra and laid on top of her. The sight of her breast was disgusting. I couldn't bear to look at them. Her scent was super feminine, and she smelled like cotton candy. I unbuckled my pants and had a hard time getting an erection. I pumped her without pulling out my penis. She pumped me back, and finally, my penis reached its full potential.

"Please go slow," she pleaded.

"Shut up. You wanted this, right?" I closed my eyes and imagined she was someone else, and with my pants still on, I pulled my penis out of my boxer's and jammed it into her vagina. She screamed a loud but calm scream. I hated to feel her insides. It felt like unhealed warm guts. I pumped hard and harder.

"Please slow down, Damien. Please," she begged.

"It's almost over, Brianna," I said as I jammed her 3 more times before I stopped. The encounter was more painful for me than maybe it was for her. I didn't enjoy it, and I couldn't believe I had lost my virginity to her. She laid still and silent. I had accomplished my goal. I stripped her of her innocence, and in return, she would hate Dawn and me. I started quickly packing up.

"Please wait for me to get dressed. I'm scared,"

Brianna said as she rushed to find her bra

"Hurry up!" I rudely responded.

I walked super fast out of the field, and she fastly walked behind me. I didn't even bother walking her home. When we exited the field, she walked her way, and I walked mines. We didn't even say good night. I felt dirty, and so did she. I'm sure she felt violated, and so did I. I didn't think about how this plan would affect me when I decided to invade Brianna's body and never speak to her again. All I wanted was a shower and to forget what had happened.

"Back the fuck up! I have a gun!" I yelled to Mr. Ralph.

"I told you to leave her alone. Didn't I tell you!" he screamed.

"You can't tell me what to do, you pervert. At least I didn't rape her."

"I still know your secret. Or did you forget? I'm not dead! You are!

"I hate you!" I screamed as I shot Mr. Ralph in the head. He just poofed away.

I woke up sweaty and frantic. I heard a bunch of screaming downstairs in the living room. I stretched and wiped the crust out of my eyes. I walked to the bathroom and took a leak. My penis was sore, which reminded me of what I had done with Brianna the night before. I heard more chaos as I flushed the toilet. I grabbed my toothbrush when I heard Mama call my name. I placed the toothbrush back in the holder and walked towards the steps.

"Get down here now! Right now, Damien!"

"Mama, what's wrong? Dag!" I asked as I started coming down the steps. There were at least ten people in our living room.

"Damien, have you seen Brianna? Have you seen my baby?" Brianna's mother asked with a crackling voice as tears rolled down her cheeks.

"Seen her when? What is going on?" I asked in a defensive tone.

"Damien, I told them you were supposed to meet Brianna last night. Sorry for snitching, but no one has seen her," Dawn said with tears in her eyes.

"Please tell the truth. My Baby is missing. My only child. My sweet, sweet baby!" Brianna's mother cried in her husband's arms as everyone looked at me for answers.

Damien, we are waiting. What happened?" Mama asked with a look of disappointment and embarrassment all over her face.

"What do you mean missing? She didn't come home?" I asked.

"No! Now tell us what the fuck happened!" her father demanded.

"Calm down. Damien is still a child. He's my child. Let's hear him out," Mama said.

"I'm so confused. Me and Brianna went to the field last night, and Uhm," I started to explain.

"And what?" Brianna's father launched at me with his fist balled up. Everyone grabbed him right before he reached me, and I fell on the steps.

"That's it! Everyone get out of my house!" Mama yelled.

"We are not leaving until he tells us where our daughter is," Brianna's mother said calmly but firmly.

"I don't know! After the field, she walked her way, and I walked mines. Shit, I should've walked her home," I said in an explanatory tone.

"Boy, watch your mouth!" Mama yelled.

"So you telling us, you haven't seen her since you left the field? I'm calling the police back. You will tell me what you did to my daughter. If she is hurt in any way, I will kill you myself. That's a promise," Brianna's father said as he grabbed his wife to go.

"Please, Damien. Please, tell me. Where is my Baby?" Brianna's mother cried as her father grabbed her.

"I swear on everything, I don't know. I didn't see Brianna again," I said with sympathy in my voice.

Everyone left the house in slow motion. All the neighbors looked at me with disgust. I couldn't believe

Dawn threw me under the bus like that. More importantly, what happened to Brianna. I know I couldn't recall killing Mr. Ralph, but surely I know I didn't hurt Brianna. I knew I didn't have a blackout because I remember walking home. Mama asked me a thousand questions, and she seemed more annoyed that my story stayed the same. Mama looked at Dawn as she just cried and cried. She was devastated, and

Dawn looked at me as if I was a monster. Strangely Mama didn't console Dawn. It's almost like she ignored her. I guess I was her main focus, and she couldn't hide how she felt towards me. I already felt regret for my encounter with Brianna, but now I regretted everything. It wasn't long before the police were knocking at the door. It happened to be the same detective that arrested Papa; apparently, our neighborhood was his district. I was nervous, and Mama was a wreck.

"Hi Damien, Nice to see you again. I'm sorry we are meeting on bad terms again, but I have some questions for you," Detective Ross stated.

"Hi, Detective Ross. I swear I didn't do anything to Brianna. I wish I knew where she was. Everyone is accusing me of something I didn't do. All I did last night was lose my virginity," I sang like a bird. I talked so fast, I barely knew what I said.

"Slow down, Damien. We'll get this straight. We

just want to find her. You are not in trouble, but I need to know everything you did yesterday. Let's start with the time you arrived back from seeing your father," Detective Ross stated with firmness.

"Does he need a lawyer? He is still a minor," Mama interrupted.

"A lawyer? Mama, I didn't do anything! I will tell you everything, Detective Ross," I complied in an explanatory tone.

"Ma'am, he is not under arrest, nor are we accusing him of anything. We just want to ask him a few questions down the station. Of course, you can be present at all times during the interview."

"I don't like this. Nor do I trust y'all to properly do your job. My husband is innocently arrested right now for nothing!" Mama blurted out.

"I think it's odd we would be back here within a few months too. By law, you can have a lawyer present. For now, we just want to find Brianna," Detective Ross stated, ignoring Mama's jabs.

"Why can't you ask the questions right here?" Mama asked.

"Brianna is missing. All information is crucial. If something comes up in her missing case, the station will have a recording to reflect back on."

"Mama, it's okay. We can go to the station," I interjected to calm Mama down.

Mama and I entered the cold police station. The detectives sat us in a dark and gloomy room, similar to those I had seen in movies. Mama appeared more frightened than me, her legs trembled under the metal table, and she couldn't keep still. I watched her eyes wander the room and occasionally look at me. Surprisingly Mama gave me a look of sympathy, not her usual" Why Damien? Why?" look. I, too, was fearful, but I knew I hadn't hurt Brianna. I just prayed she would show up at any moment. Detective Ross walked in with a Pepsi in his hand as his oversized suit hung recklessly over his boney shoulders.

"Would you like something to drink, Damien?" he asked with a friendly grin. "You know we are starting to see a lot of each other lately. I've been replaying something your father said to me the day we arrested him. But no way that can be true," he burst out laughing as he handed me the Pepsi.

"Detective Ross, I'm not sure what my father said to you or what happened to Brianna. All I know is I didn't do anything to her," I explained.

"How did you get to the field with Brianna?" he asked as he sipped his soda.

"We already had plans to hook up that night. Soon as Mama and Brianna went to sleep, I went to Brianna's, and she came outside with me."

"She willingly walked out her front door?" he

questioned.

"No, she jumped out of her bedroom window, and we went to the field to, you know?" I stated, trying to avoid the details.

"No, we don't know," Mama sarcastically stated.

"We had sex!" I shamefully blurted out.

"After the sex, what happened?" Detective Ross asked.

"Nothing. We didn't like it, so we didn't speak. We left the field, and I walked my way home, and she walked hers. I swear that's the last time I saw her."

"So, you didn't even walk her home. See Damien, I want to believe you, but I'm having a hard time understanding how you were the last person with her, and she didn't make it home."

"I don't understand either," I admitted.

"Can we leave now? He doesn't know anything else," Mama asked as she grabbed her purse.

"For now, you can leave, but I may have more questions later, so be available. Hopefully, this is just a misunderstanding, and Brianna turns up soon," Detective Ross said as he opened up the door in the interrogation room.

Mama and I left in silence. There was nothing to say. I had conflicted emotions. I should have felt sympathy, but I didn't. I felt confused and wrongly accused, but I couldn't find compassion for Brianna's disappearance. I never wanted anything to happen to her, but it made me mad that something happened to her after she was with me.

Mama acted strange the entire ride home. She talked about dinner and random things that made no sense. She completely ignored the elephant in the car. Mama looked tired and stressed. We returned home, and that fast, there were missing posters all over the neighborhood. Mama simply said, "Like Detective Ross said, hopefully, this is a misunderstanding, and she will turn up soon."

8
THE LAST DAY

"Get your filthy hands off me," Brianna screamed as I held her down.

"Be quiet before someone hears you. I just need you to tell everyone you are okay," I said as I slowly removed my hand from Brianna's mouth.

"No one will hear her. She's dead. You killed her like you killed me," Mr. Ralph said as he walked super fast towards Brianna and me.

"I did not kill her! I did not! You go away! This is not about you," I screamed.

"I will always be here. I might have had some evil little girl desires, but at least I wasn't a murderer like you!" Mr. Ralph screamed, walking closer to me with a knife in his hand.

"I did not kill her!"

I woke up to Mama's warm hands shaking me and calling my name. Since Brianna's disappearance, the nightmares had gotten worse. It had been three days and no sign of Brianna. After the interrogation at the police station, I've been staying up all night until my body finally falls asleep from exhaustion. I knew I had a sense of evil inside me, but I wondered if I was really capable of murder. I blocked the thoughts out. They would do me no good.

Mama told me to just wait for Brianna to show up, and this would all be over. For once, I listened. Mama and I relationship had actually grown over the last few days. I guess a mother always loves her child, and when they really need their mother, she'll be there. Dawn has been acting extremely weird since the disappearance of Brianna. I know it was her best friend, but she even stopped eating. All she does is stay in her room, pout and complain about how bored or lonely she is.

The morning moved slowly. I sat at the kitchen table as Mama finished up breakfast. She called Dawn multiple times with no answer. She suggested we just go ahead and eat. It actually shocked me that Mama would eat without her precious Dawn. Maybe she was just giving her space, but something was off with them two. I picked up the fork to taste the first bite of eggs when we heard a loud knock at the door.

"I'll get it," Mama said as she threw her napkin on the table. "Who is it?" she asked in an annoyed tone.

"Open this door before I kick it down!" Brianna's mother screamed.

"Look, I've been patient with you, and I've felt your pain, but you will not keep threatening me," Mama said as she opened the door.

"Ralph's house was burnt down late last night, and they believe Brianna was inside. Why did you do this to my Baby?" Brianna's mom yelled from the doorway towards me.

"Mrs. Scottsdale, we asked you not to come here. We told you multiple times not to interfere with our investigation. We are handling it. We promise you we will solve Brianna's disappearance. Please go back home," Detective Ross said as he grabbed Brianna's mother's arm and began walking her away from our house.

"I can't believe this is happening. I'm sure his slinky ass will be back with more questions," Mama said, referring to detective Ross as she slammed the front door.

"Mama, you know I never left this house. I would never hurt Brianna. I can't believe she's dead," I said as Dawn walked into the kitchen.

"Dead? Brianna is dead? You killed her! You killed my best friend! You fucking maniac, I told you to stay away," Dawn yelled as she entered the kitchen. She then launched at me with punches and kicks.

"I didn't kill your slutty friend. Don't you ever put your hands on me, you little snitch," I said as I pushed Dawn away as she continued to swing at the air.

"Stop it! I won't have my own kids fighting each other. It's enough people against us. Hell, the entire neighborhood hates us. Everybody sit down and eat this damn breakfast I've prepared!" Mama screamed and slammed Dawn's plate at the table.

We ate in silence. The only sound in the room was the sound of the forks touching the plates. We intensely looked at one another with thoughts that should never leave one's mind. I wanted to punch Dawn in the throat for attacking me. Dawn wanted me to pay for the murder of her friend, and Mama was tired. She was tired of the drama, the fighting, the lies, and the accusations. Her face looked drained, and her once beautiful smile was depleted. Her new face was a face of worry and doubt.

All I could think about was who would burn down Mr. Ralph's house. My next thought was, how did Brianna get there? My thoughts were racing, and I felt more confused than ever. I couldn't comprehend what was happening. I weirdly wanted to talk to Papa. I wanted to ask him about jail. How was it? Would I get raped? Was it like the movies? I knew I would be blamed for Brianna's death. I started preparing for the inevitable. I lost my train of thought as I heard an outburst from Dawn.

"So, where did they find her? Can someone at least tell me that?" Dawn demanded.

"Her mother said they believe she was in Mr. Ralph's house, which someone burnt down last night. That's all we know, right now," Mama said.

"Dawn, I know you didn't want me with Brianna that day, but I didn't hurt her. I never left this house last night to set a fire. Please trust me, Dawn. You are my twin, and you know me better than anyone," I pleaded.

"I don't know you at all. Why is Papa in jail? Huh? Tell Mama," Dawn coldly responded.

"This is not about Papa. This is about you thinking I'm a killer. I know I'm not perfect, but come on, be for real. Do you really think I murdered your best friend just to agitate you?" I asked.

"All I know is, she was with you, and now she is gone. You talked with the cops, and now Papa is gone. Who's next, Damien?" Dawn asked with sarcasm.

"Ok, now Dawn, that's enough?" Mama said.

"Dawn, you can think what you want, but I didn't do anything to Brianna. I'm telling the truth," I said in a sincere tone.

"This is too much for me. I can't take this anymore.

We are going to move out. Get the hell away from this neighborhood. I don't want to hear another word about Brianna, Ralph, or any of this stuff. Leave it right here in this house. We can go stay with Sheryl," Mama said sternly, taking control of the conversation.

We started packing immediately. Aunt Sheryl lived in the house Mama's parents left behind when they died. Mama always felt the place should've been left for her. Mama always popped in and visited whenever she pleased without announcing herself. Aunt Sheryl couldn't stand Mama, but Mama felt it was her house too.

Mama once told us that Aunt Sheryl thought every woman in the family was a whore. She believed Mama was a whore, and Papa paid her for sex, even to this day. We knew for sure Aunt Sheryl wouldn't be pleased with a family of three moving in with her unexpectedly. She wasn't the nice aunt that baked cookies when you arrived. She was the aunt you dreaded seeing.

Aunt Sheryl's house was old and creaky. It hadn't been remodeled or updated since my grandparents died. When we visited last summer, it smelled of old people's armpits and mothballs. The paint was cracked and had a dusty brown color from the cigarette smoke over the years. Everything happened so fast, I had to take a minute to absorb the move.

We were leaving the only house we ever knew, all the memories, laughter, and even the tragedies. Dawn and I learned how to walk in this house, and we constantly played on the steps as little kids. We knew running wouldn't solve our problems. We also knew it would look suspicious leaving out of the blue. Mama said none of us was under arrest, and we could do as we pleased.

A few hours later, I went into Dawn's room. Dawn finally started talking to me again as she packed. I guess she was lonely or needed to express her frustrations with someone, even if it was her murderous brother. Dawn was stressed, she loved our house, but she especially loved her room. After venting about moving, she came and hugged me tight and cried in my arms. This vulnerable side of Dawn made me love her more than myself at times. I rubbed my hands through her semi chopped off hair and squeezed her back tight. No matter what, Dawn was my twin, and we shared a bond that even murder couldn't break.

I still knew in my heart I wasn't a killer. I still couldn't remember hurting anyone. As I rubbed Dawn's hair, it had such a smell. It was a smell I had never encountered on her. It almost smelled like chemicals. I sniffed harder as she cried louder. I felt her drool dripping from her bottom lip as she sobbed.

I became obsessed with the smell. I couldn't understand why her hair smelled of anything other than shampoo.

The more I smelled it, the dizzier I became. I then began to question if I was smelling anything at all. Everything in my life was starting to feel like an illusion. Just as I leaned in to take one last sniff, Dawn let me go. I often wondered who Dawn was? I felt I barely knew her. She played many characters, and I couldn't figure out who she really was. Around our parents, she was quiet and innocent. With her friends, she cursed and bossed everyone around. With me, she loved to push my buttons.

I decided to stand against the wall in silence and watch her every move. I felt like I left my body and entered hers. I watched her walk around the bedroom, picking up old items that had sentimental value to her. She seemed so upset about the move, but the longer I watched her, the more I realized she wasn't who I thought she was. Actually, I didn't know who she was at all. The image I had of Dawn in my mind is not who appeared in front of me. I couldn't see her soul through her eyes. All I could see was fakeness.

"Why are you sitting there watching me like a stalker instead of packing? Mama said we had to be gone in two hours," Dawn asked, snapping me back to my reality.

"Dawn, I can't see your soul through your eyes. It's so weird. Every time I look at you, all I see is a pretender," I admitted.

"Oh my God. Did you smoke some weed again? Whenever you do that stuff, you start talking about eyes and souls and craziness," Dawn asked as she shook her head.

"I did smoke. I had a half of blunt from before. Everything looks so strange, especially you. I can see things when I'm high. I'm not crazy. The truth is within the eyes," I said in a defensive tone.

"Boy, if you can't see my soul, then you are clearly crazy!" Dawn said as she taped up another box.

"Dawn, you can't possibly be the perfect person that you portray to be. We all have some sort of darkness, even if it's only our thoughts."

"Yes, Damien. I do sometimes think crazy shit, but I don't act on it. No one said I was perfect. You think that. You've made up who you think I am in your mind," Dawn said in an annoyed tone.

"Well, who are you?" I bluntly asked.

"I'm Dawn. I'm a girl who was birthed with a retarded brother who won't let me pack because he smoked some weed. Now he decided to come into my room asking me a bunch of dumb shit while my best friend is possibly dead. Nice to meet you. And you are?" Dawn sarcastically asked.

"I'm Damien, the retarded brother who finally sees right through the girl he was birthed with, who appears so perfect, but is not."

I walked to my bedroom and felt stuck. I was extremely paranoid, and I couldn't get Dawn or Brianna out of my mind. The weed I smoked, I had for about six months. I got it from a guy who sells it around the school. The first time I smoked, I accused Dawn of being the devil. It took forever for the high to go away. I said I would never smoke again, and Dawn agreed. I decided to smoke today because I was stressed about moving and being accused of doing something to Brianna. I wanted to escape my reality in any way possible.

I replayed the night with Brianna, and I almost got sick to my stomach. I had no right to steal her innocence and throw her away like garbage, just to have Dawn to myself. I could see her happy face when I knocked on the window. She turned on the light, and her highly pink room lit up. Brianna's hair was perfectly in place, and she smiled so hard when she saw it was me. I can see her smile over and over again.

I tried to remember if I saw anyone else outside that night. I pictured going back to that night in my mind to see if I remembered anything. I didn't see anyone, not a car ride by, a person in the window, or a random guy walking down the street. Detective Ross said, "*eighty percent of missing cases come from people they know.*" I started thinking maybe Brianna's father did something to her. Brianna was overdeveloped. What if he was sneaking into having sex with her. Perhaps, what I did pushed her over the edge, and she threatened to tell. I realized that was just a stupid theory. Her father didn't seem like a pervert.

Honestly, after I left her, anything could have happened. It's just such a mystery of what did happen. After we leave this house, Mama said no more talk of these things, and I'm happy about that. I realized I wasted an hour stuck on my bed, high, tired, and overthinking. Dawn burst into my room.

"I knew you were in here doing nothing. Come on, get up! I'll help you pack," Dawn said, grabbing a box off the floor as she looked for the tape gun.

"Thanks. Good ole perfect Dawn always come to save the show. I knew you were coming to help me. It was the right thing to do, and you always do the right thing. I'll play along," I said as I handed Dawn the tape gun.

"Ouch, what the hell is this?" Dawn yelled, pulling the unfamiliar wood stick from under my bed.

"I don't know where it came from. I almost stepped on it one morning. Do you know how it got in here?" I asked, looking deep into Dawn's eyes.

"No. But it's kind of creepy. I would get rid of it if

I were you, especially if you don't know where it came from.

"Honestly, I don't know why I kept it. I just threw it under my bed and forgot about it.

"But, you are such a neat freak; how could you forget about it? It really doesn't make any sense, Damien."

"Dawn, I'm high! Nothing makes sense to me right now. Just trash it," I demanded.

We finished packing, and it wasn't long before it was time to leave the house that we so dearly loved. We walked through the house saying our goodbyes as Mama waited at the bottom of the steps for us. She held her head low. She wore a big pair of sunglasses to hide her tears. We opened the door and left our house as a family. We thought we had a chance for a new start. Unfortunately, where we were going was much worse, and problems didn't just disappear as Brianna did.

9
TIRED

"Please stop. I'm only a child," I pleaded.

"You are not a child, you are an adult now, and things will never be right until you tell what you did," Mr. Ralph said with a sinister grin.

"How are you back? I asked in confusion.

"I never left and never will. Do you want to know what I did to your little friend Brandon, as you call him?" Mr. Ralph asked with holes in his face.

"What did you do? What is his name?" I questioned.

"Damien, wake up. Are you still having those nightmares?" Mama asked as she handed me a glass of water.

"How do you know? I never told you I had bad dreams," I questioned.

"Boy, I know everything about you, now get up and go eat. I made you and Dawn a big breakfast," Mama said as she caressed my right arm.

"Mama, are you okay? You look a little off. Is Aunt Sheryl threatening to put us out again?" I asked Mama.

"Damien, just stay out of her way. Listen to what she tells you and ignore her nasty ways. Time will go by fast, and this will all be the past," Mama said as she rubbed my arm a little more.

"Are you sure you're okay? Why are you so dressed up?"

"I was feeling ugly. I decided to wake up, get dressed, feel pretty, and cook a good meal for my kids. I made all your favorites."

"Oh, you made your famous biscuits? You should've been told me that!" I said as I got out of the bed, stretched, and reached for Mama's hand to join me.

"Go ahead and eat; I already ate. I cooked almost everything in the fridge, so I'm heading to the market. Wake Dawn up for me too," Mama said as she watched me walk out of my room. I wondered why she sat on my bed, looking puzzled, but I just left the room and went to get Dawn.

Dawn and I sat at the table with Aunt Sheryl, eating

as if it was our last meal. Aunt Sheryl was not an easy sight to see early in the morning. She was a heavier woman who wore an oversized T-shirt that said, "WELCOME TO LAS VEGAS." She wore it just about every day, except the one day a month she decided to wash her ass. We always joked about how we didn't believe she's actually been to Vegas. She smelled like stale cigarettes and mothballs. Her breath and her armpits nearly killed me every time I was in her presence. Her hair was matted, and her fishy vagina was an instant man-killer. We had been living with this disgrace of a woman for precisely three years before Mama decided to make this significant breakfast none of us would ever forget.

Dawn and I had become closer over the last two years. I think we had no choice. It was us against the scum in the house. Something felt off as we continued to eat breakfast. I wondered why Mama wouldn't eat with us since she cooked so much food. She made bacon, ham, eggs, pancakes, french toast, grits, and fried potatoes. Mama never makes two portions of meat and two starches, not even on our birthdays. For a split second, I wondered if Mama poisoned us. She hated her sister, and she sometimes hated me, and ever since we moved, she's been acting weird towards Dawn. They are not as close as they once were. Mama sometimes even seems to like me more. Just as I wondered, *were we all eating to our death*, Mama appeared.

"Okay, guys, I'm going to the market, and I may be out a while because I cooked up everything," Mama said in a joking tone.

"Okay," I mumbled with food in my mouth.

"Get me a carton of cigarettes, would you?" Aunt Sheryl asked with eggs falling from her mouth.

"Yeah, I can bring you some back. See you later, Dawn," Mama said as she turned to walk away.

"See you, Mama, I love you," Dawn said while putting her cup of juice back on the table.

"Love you all too. See you soon," Mama smiled as she shut the front door behind her.

"Going to the market, my ass. Looks like she is going to be a married whore. No woman gets all dressed up to go to the damn market. She thinks we are stupid. Well, you two are stupid. Hurry up and eat so you can clean up my kitchen," Aunt Sheryl said soon as Mama left.

"My mother is not a whore!" Dawn exclaimed.

"Awwww, did I upset you? Don't worry. You will walk right in her footsteps. A little whore in the making. I see how you look at my friend when he comes over," Aunt Sheryl said, looking Dawn up and down as she lit a cigarette.

"He only comes over once a month when you get

your social security check. Leave my sister alone. We will clean up your kitchen," I interrupted.

"Who the fuck do you think you are talking to? Your little ass might be sleeping outside tonight. I never wanted y'all here anyway!" Aunt Sheryl yelled.

Seven hours had passed, and no word from Mama. Aunt Sheryl refused to let us use the house phone to call the police. She kept saying, Mama was somewhere getting fucked, so don't worry. I was two steps from chopping that Bitch head off. I knew if one more person got hurt around me, I would for sure be in jail. Detective Ross was still doing random pop-ups. It didn't take long for him to find us. No one was ever charged for the disappearance of Brianna. Mr. Ralph's house burnt to a crisp, and there was no evidence. I knew I had to be careful, but this pissy aunt of mines was pushing my last buttons.

I finally decided to go to sleep, and if Mama wasn't home in the morning, I would surely find a way to call the police. I showered and lay in my bed. I tucked my hands under the pillow to fluff it up, and I felt a piece of paper neatly folded. I grabbed the paper and slowly unfolded it. I felt butterflies in my stomach and knew the words on the paper would somehow change my life forever. I sat up on the end of the bed, the letter read

Damien,

I'm sure by now you are wondering where I am. You act like you are so tough, but I know you have a good heart. I'm sure that Bitch of a sister of mine has already started talking trash. I hate to write these words, but I'm gone. I can't do this anymore. I've tried to raise you and Dawn the best I knew how, and it got harder when Papa left. I haven't been the same since we left our house and moved in with the Devil. You may be wondering how I could leave y'all with her? I asked myself the same question at least a hundred times. I decided you both could handle her. If I don't know anything, I know my kids don't take no shit. I'm not sure what happened to Brianna a few years ago, but I know in my gut you didn't hurt her. I just wanted you to know that. Before I decided to be a coward and leave you both, I reflected on my time as your mother, and it was either kill myself or leave. I chose to leave. You might not have a mother right there, but you have a mother still alive. Break the news easy to Dawn. Be there for her as she is truly lost without you. And being lost is not a good place for her. Love you both and tell your aunt I'll send money monthly.

PS. I get nightmares too! The only time I didn't get them was when Papa and I went away alone every year. Keep fighting them.

I balled the letter up and threw it on the floor. I felt

an instant strike of betrayal fill my insides. My heart raced with anxiety, and I felt a peck of sweat embrace my forehead. I paced back and forth as my mind rambled with thoughts of deceit. I knew I couldn't tell Dawn right away. She was too fragile. I slowly walked to the balled-up piece of paper and re-read Mama's letter about fifteen times. The more I read it, the more I wanted to rip her fucking head off.

I was angry and frustrated, but I was sympathetic. My emotions were unpredictable and unruly. I never imagined Mama not being in my life. I was upset I wouldn't have her motherly love in my presence. It didn't matter what evil lived inside of me; she was my mother. She had a moral commitment as my mother, and she was obligated to love me unconditionally.

I couldn't understand why she mentioned the nightmares at such a time. I imagined Mama writing the letter as I sat at the table enjoying her big breakfast. I pictured her rubbing my arm to awaken me from the terror of Mr. Ralph. I never knew Mama had nightmares, and it made me curious. I even wondered what she had done in her life to have evil haunt her during the misty night. I am, in fact, her child. What if she was the evil that lived inside of me? I immediately disregarded that thought. Mama's heart was pure, and no way had she done anything to harm a living creature. I then wondered how she could leave us with this Bitch of an aunt. My thoughts rambled until I finally fell asleep around 3 a.m.

At 5:10 a.m., I was abruptly awoken with cold ice water thrown all over my body. It gave me an instant chill. I felt an ice cube under my armpit and threw it on the floor. I felt like I was still dreaming, or should I say, having another nightmare. I was restless and discombobulated. I rubbed my hands along my face to ensure I was awake. I felt water drops against my smooth skin. The chill from the water immersed my body. I finally came to the reality that I wasn't asleep. The winter chill from my cracked window in the room was even more proof that someone had insulted me.

"Get your lazy ass up. Your skank of a mother didn't return. I need some cigarettes and some snacks," Aunt Sheryl screamed in my face.

"Why did you throw water on me?" I asked while removing my soaking wet shirt.

"The truth is, I just wanted to. I really don't like you or that little thang that looks like you. She is my least favorite of all. Your mother had some nerve coming here after what happened when we were younger. Never mind that, get dressed."

"What happened when you were younger? Get dressed for what? It's five in the morning."

"I said never mind. Get dressed to go get my cigarettes. By any chance, have you heard from your mother?" Aunt Sheryl asked, now standing in the doorway smoking a cigarette.

"No! It's still dark outside. Can I get your cigarettes later?" I asked after lying about not hearing from Mama.

"Let me find out you are afraid of the dark," She laughed. "Well, I can put it this way, you can take your ass now, or you can wait for the light. But be prepared to sleep outside on the porch tonight for making me wait," Aunt Sheryl smiled as she handed me a balled-up twenty-dollar bill. The balled-up money instantly made me think of Mama's note. It made me furious all over again.

"I don't think it's smart to wake me up this way anymore. I'm not who you think I am, and it's best you don't have to know who I really am," I said as I snatched the note.

"Well, I can show you who I am right now! Right now," Aunt Sheryl said as she raised her big arm, her skin hung like her saggy breast. The funk from her underarms grew as her arm raised, and there were her five fingers landing on my still-wet face.

"Ouch," I pierced as I fell back without completely falling.

"Now, for starting all this drama this morning, your punishment will be no breakfast," Aunt Sheryl said as she turned to walk away.

I think I was more upset that I expressed my pain aloud. I let her know she hurt me, which caused a rage in me that I couldn't control. I wanted to kill her at that very moment. Not only did she slap me, she hadn't bathed in months. Who knows what was on her filthy hands. I was sixteen now, and I could have clearly kicked her ass with no problem. I ran to the bathroom and washed my face. Dawn came running to the bathroom behind me.

"Did you hear from Mama? Did she call?" Dawn excitedly asked.

"No. Forget about Mama, Dawn," I said in a low, irritated tone.

"What happened to you? What did Aunt Sheryl do now?" Dawn asked, trying to look at my face.

"The big Bitch slapped me. Can you believe that? Has she hit you before?"

"No, but she told me she would stick a broomstick up my slut ass if I disobeyed her again."

"Dawn, I hate to tell you this. Mama is gone. She's not coming back. All we have is each other now."

"What do you mean? Mama would never just leave us. Especially not with her. She knows how bad Aunt Sheryl treats us," Dawn whispered.

"Little Ugly Boy. Are you finished crying? I'm still waiting for my cigarettes," Aunt Sheryl yelled from downstairs.

"Dawn, I don't have time to explain right now. Mama is safe, but she left us. Did that monster just call me ugly? I'm one second away from killing her ass," I mumbled to Dawn.

"Don't say that. Just go get her cigarettes, and I'll start her breakfast. You can tell me more about Mama later," Dawn whispered as she left the bathroom.

I walked to the store in the blistering cold. I felt the wind smack my face, similar to the smack Aunt Sheryl just gave me. I thought of Mama and smiled. When Dawn and I were younger, Mama never let us go out on cold days like this. She made us pancakes and hot chocolate. Sometimes we would walk around the house with blankets and watch movies. It was amazing snuggling up. Papa was never home on these cold days. I wondered where he was. My warm memory faded as I entered the store. I got back to Aunt Sheryl's and smelled the food from the front door. I was excited to eat. Aunt Sheryl refused to give us dinner because she said we had a big breakfast from Mama. So, we went to bed hungry.

"Here's your cigarettes and snacks. Can I go eat now?" I asked as I handed the bag to Aunt Sheryl.

"I don't know what you are going to eat. You took so long that I ate your share. Don't worry, you can eat at dinner time," Aunt Sheryl said as she snatched the bag from me.

"I didn't have dinner last night, and now no breakfast?" I asked in a sarcastic tone.

"Damien! Come help me clean these dishes, please," Dawn yelled from the kitchen.

"Yeah, Damien. Go help her clean up, my little slave. When you finish, go wash those loads of clothes and scrub that bathroom floor," Aunt Sheryl demanded. I ignored her and walked to the kitchen.

"I have this for you. I saved half of my food for you. If Mama is really gone, we will have to look after each other," Dawn said, handing me a napkin with a bit of food on it.

"Thanks, Dawn, I was so hungry. I'm glad she fed you at least."

"She didn't. I snuck this as I was cooking her meal. I had a feeling she wasn't going to feed us. So, tell me more about Mama. I'm confused. How do you know she's not coming back?" Dawn asked with curiosity. I hurriedly swallowed the piece of pancake Dawn gave me and handed her the letter.

To my surprise, after Dawn read the letter, she just calmly handed it back to me. We decided to stick together and make sure we both got food. We knew we didn't want to go to foster care. Dawn started reaching out to our aunt Lily on Papa's side. Aunt Lily would speak to Dawn but would hang up whenever I got on the phone. Papa had convinced her that I made their brother, Uncle Robby, a mute. Aunt Lily didn't like me, and she made it clear, but she loved Dawn.

Everyone loved Dawn except Aunt Sheryl. Actually, she disliked Dawn more than she disliked me. She degraded her, day in and day out. She said she was a slut and something evil was inside of her. Aunt Sheryl eventually started slapping Dawn too. I was losing my patience with Aunt Sheryl, and Dawn knew it.

Aunt Sheryl had no friends, so she would talk to the mail lady when she could. Often, the mail lady would try to avoid her, but her luck ran out at times, and she had to deal with the stench of our gossiping aunt. I heard the mail truck pull up, and I found myself hoping we would get mail from Mama. We never did. Dawn rarely talked about Mama, and she didn't look for her after a few weeks. I heard Aunt Sheryl open the front door. I stood in the shadow of the dining room with my ears pierced to the door to listen.

"Hey Girl, I missed you the last couple of runs. How are you?" Aunt Sheryl asked in a kissing ass tone.

"Hey, Sheryl. I've been alright. Just working. How about you?" the mail lady asked, uninterested.

"Girl, it's been a mess. My sluty, I meant promiscuous sister, left her two damn kids here. Can you believe that?" Aunt Sheryl asked in full gossip mode.

"What? She just left them? Did you make sure she's okay?" The mail lady asked in a concerned tone.

"She's okay. She runs away from her shit. She did the same thing when we were young. She stole my man and ran off."

"Dag, Sheryl. I'm sorry to hear that. That's big of you to forgive her," the mail lady said as she fumbled through her mail.

"I didn't forgive her. She just showed up here with her kids. Not to mention these are kids by a man that she stole from me—the nerve of some people. I was dating Jerome first, and Girl, he is fine. He is a tall glass of sexiness. The next thing I knew, they were going out behind my back. I heard he was paying her for sex," Aunt Sheryl said in a matter-fact tone.

"Well, he married her, and they had kids. You may need to let that go. I'm kind of," the mail lady said before Aunt Sheryl cut her off.

"Let it go. What do you know? These should be my kids, not hers. I should've been his wife, not her. Then she runs off to leave me with her bastard kids. And that little girl, she is the worse of them all. I can see right through her. She's an evil little whore," Aunt Sheryl ranted.

"Sheryl, I really have to go finish my runs. You know how busy Mondays are," the mail lady said as she rushed down the steps to get away from the house.

"Ok, Girl, I'll see you in a few days," Aunt Sheryl yelled.

I hurried up and ran to the kitchen. If I hadn't thought Aunt Sheryl was insane before, she sure did just prove it. She had to be mentally ill to think Papa would have wanted her over Mama. Even in her younger days, Aunt Sheryl was a mess. She had her old prom picture hung up in the living room that she often bragged about. It was a frightful image to see.

Aunt Sheryl wore a blue dress with red lipstick everywhere except her lips. There was lipstick on all her top teeth as she posed for the photo. She had enough hair under her underarms to make a ponytail. Mama, on the other hand, was voted prom queen. I'm sure there was never a chance Papa would've chosen Aunt Sheryl over Mama. Now it was clear to me why she hated Mama so much.

"Damien! There are no free rides around here, boy. Grab that Epsom salt, and come rub my feet!" Aunt Sheryl yelled.

10
THE FALL

"I can't breathe," I begged as I gasped for air.

"Neither can I. You killed me, remember?"

"Brianna, I didn't kill you. I fucked you, but I didn't kill you," I pleaded as her hands choked me harder.

"You killed us both. I'm tired of rotting away. Tell the truth, Damien," Brianna said as she slammed my head in the concrete.

"Well, you did kill me. How long do you think you can keep your secret? You're getting older, and it's getting harder to hide," Mr. Ralph said as he walked towards me with a shotgun.

Right as Mr. Ralph put his index finger on the trigger, I woke up to a screeching scream. It pained my ears. It was the sound of something drastically changing. I've heard this sound before. It was the sound of misery, or it could be the sound right before someone's death. It's such a precise sound of base in someone's voice when they are enduring pain. It made me excited. I jumped up, and for the first time in years, I skipped brushing my teeth. I immediately ran to the sound that was welcoming my ears as joy. I stood at the top of the steps and looked down as I saw Aunt Sheryl's body twisted like a pretzel.

I finally saw one of her eyelids close and reopen; therefore, she was alive. She lay there with big eyes filled with hurt and fear. I comforted her with a smile. I walked to the bathroom, brushed my teeth, and brushed the waves in my hair for about five minutes. I went to the little box of a room Dawn had been sleeping in, and she was snoring. I was happy she was asleep, so I could peacefully deal with Aunt Sheryl. I thought of taking a pillow and putting it over her ugly face and suffocating every ounce of oxygen from her fat ass body. That thought quickly left when I realized if I killed her, Dawn and I would become kids of the state.

Mama's neglectful ass still hadn't returned, and there was no way I was going to be placed into the system. At that moment, I decided to torture the Bitch. I knew no one would come checking for her. The mail lady would be relieved not to see her, and she surely wouldn't inquire where she was. The one man who came around only came on her check day, and he only called a week before. Well, luckily for us, she had just got her check, so that left me with three weeks to have fun.

"You fucked up now Bitch! You allowed your dumb ass self to fall down the steps," I said as I walked down the first step.

"Mmmmmmm, Mmmmm," Aunt Sheryl groaned.

"Mmmmmmm, Mmmmm what? Are you in pain? Would you like me to call you an ambulance?" I asked in a sarcastic tone.

"Mmmmmm!" She loudly nodded. Her eyes were big with excitement, like a kid being offered an ice cream before dinner.

"Bitch, you must be crazy. You think I'm actually going to get you help? No one loves you. Isn't that what you told us? No one loved us. You do know that no one is going to check on you or call. Soooooo, I could just leave you here for weeks," I grinned as I skipped down two more steps.

"Rahhhh, Mmmmmm," she pleaded without speaking one word.

"Stop all them damn animal sounds and speak.

Actually, don't speak. Your breath stinks, and it upsets my stomach," I frowned. I began to slowly sing in a mumbling voice, "Me and you are here forever. You will leave this house, Uhm, NEVER." I jumped two more steps and sang louder, "Me and you are here forever. You will leave this house, Uhm, NEVER."

I was now over the top of her body, and I saw a single salty tear roll down her cheek. I felt nothing but joy. The closer I got, the more her scent crept under my nose. It dawned on me that she would smell like death if I left her there for weeks. Her body odor was already so foul.

I looked at her crusty feet that she made me rub the day before, and I started jumping on them. I jumped up and down on her feet and ankles, and she screamed. I took my right hand and raised my arm behind my shoulder, and with speed, I smacked her face. Her cheeks were vibrating. I laughed hard and loud. She looked fearful and stunned. I slapped her again and again and again. I then started slapping her with my left hand. It was a total of seventeen smacks before I heard Dawn's footsteps creeping out of the old room she slept in.

"Damien! What are you doing? What happened?" Dawn asked in a frantic voice.

"Calm down, Dawn. She fell down the steps on her own. I just slapped her around a few times for all the shit she did to us," I explained.

"Oh, God, Damien. We will be sent to foster care. So, she just happened to have fallen down the steps? Really, Damien?" Dawn asked in a suspicious tone.

"Yes, she did. I wish I would've pushed her. Listen to me, Dawn, everything is going to be okay. I'm in control now."

"I'm not listening to you. Someone is always getting hurt around you. Yes, she is an evil woman, but Aunt Sheryl is all we have, especially since Mama," Dawn stopped mid-sentence.

"Fuck Mama Dawn," I said in a hurtful tone.

"Fuck Mama? No! Fuck you, Damien," Dawn yelled.

"Fuck me? Your twin? Listen, Dawn. I have a plan, and I just need you to follow it. This will work. Believe me."

"I don't like Aunt Sheryl either, but I won't help you do anything messed up. Let's call her an ambulance. Please, Damien. If you didn't push her, it won't be a problem. So far, all you did was smack her, right?" Dawn asked with a sincere look on her face.

"Are you listening? We are not getting this Bitch no help. We are going to feed ourselves, buy what we need, and keep her alive."

"Aunt Sheryl, can you talk?" Dawn asked from the top of the steps. Aunt Sheryl didn't respond, but instead, she started shaking uncontrollably. She wasn't having a seizure. She trembled with fear.

"Stop all that shaking. Dawn can't help you. Where is your wallet, fat girl?" I asked.

This was day one of the fall. Dawn was against my plan but made it clear she wouldn't cross me. She kept her word about us sticking together. Every time Dawn came near Aunt Sheryl, she shook uncontrollably. Since she couldn't speak for some reason, I guess she tried to show Dawn how scared she was. How pathetic? I found it odd that she couldn't talk. I couldn't understand why the fall made her lose her voice. It kind of reminded me of Uncle Robby. He lost his voice and became mute. Papa blamed me so much that I agreed to doing it. I hadn't actually taken Uncle Robby's voice. I didn't know how to take someone's voice. That's absurd.

We left Aunt Sheryl in the same spot where she fell for weeks. She smelled awful, and she would often moan in the middle of the night. She had made multiple bowel movements, and she was beyond pissy. Dawn's job was to give her toilet water but no food. Dawn kept saying she would die if we didn't give her food. After the second day, I agreed to give her cat food only.

Dawn cooked the food for us, and I monitored the money. We both avoided going up and down the steps so we wouldn't have to see or smell her. We covered our noses before entering the stairway and ran past her. Dawn often complained about being the one to feed her because she had to get close enough to give her the cat food and water, and the smell was overwhelming. I told her to start only feeding her once a day. She could stand to lose a few pounds anyway. The days were going by fast. I came up with this plan, but I hadn't decided what to do with Aunt Sheryl after the three weeks.

Although Aunt Sheryl couldn't speak, she could write. Even if we tried to fix what had been done, she could always tell that we tortured her. Well, Dawn didn't really do anything. I'm the one who tortured her. I occasionally smacked her for no reason. One night, she kept moaning, and it drove me insane. I had a hard enough time sleeping because of the nightmares. I didn't need her noise waking me up. I got up, walked down the steps, and pulled my penis out. Aunt Sheryl looked terrified.

"What do you think I'm going to do with this dick my Daddy gave me? You were in love with him, right?" I asked as I wiggled it around.

"Mmmmm," she groaned louder. Maybe hoping Dawn would hear and come save her.

"Haha. You think I would do something sexual to your pissy and shitty ass? Ha. You are crazier than I thought. I'm about to use this penis to pee all over you. Are you ready?" I asked as if she could respond.

I pissed all over her. Her face, her hair, even her crusty feet. It was so degrading, even for me. She kept her eyes closed the entire time. I knew at that moment she had regretted mistreating us. For me, that was enough to stop the torture. That was the closure I needed. There was no more I could do to her without killing her. It was no more that needed to be done. Aunt Sheryl had suffered enough. Her being bent up on the floor like a pretzel was becoming more of a burden for Dawn and me. Aunt Sheryl was lying there in her feces, urine, my urine, eating cat food every day, drinking toilet water, and losing her legs and voice was indeed enough.

The following day, I woke up and went to a medical supply store. I purchased a wheelchair for $89 and a shower seat for $49. I carried it with me on two buses. I got a carton of off-brand cigarettes off the street for $25. I spent $5 on two containers of baby wipes, and I made my way back to the house. Dawn was still asleep when I entered the house. Aunt Sheryl's smell had now made it to the front door. The guy that fucked her once a month already called once. We told him that she was at the market. We knew the following week, he would call back to start buttering her up for check day. I woke Dawn up and told her we all needed to talk. Dawn and I stood at the bottom of the steps over Aunt Sheryl's body. I could tell she thought her time had come to an end, and we were about to kill her. She was wrong.

"Look. It has been a crazy three weeks. By no means am I apologizing. You deserve everything you got. I think you learned your lesson, and it's time to move forward," I said to Aunt Sheryl with my nose covered.

"Damien, what are you talking about? It's too early for this," Dawn said as she wiped the crust from her eyes.

"I'm talking about making an agreement that benefits everyone. Here's the deal, Sheryl. Your name is Sheryl now. I think we can all agree; there's no need to acknowledge you as our aunt anymore.

"Sheryl, it is," Dawn replied.

"Sheryl, listen up. We will pick you up off the floor, clean you up, put you in that wheelchair over there, give you cigarettes, food, and beer. We will park you in front of the TV, where you stayed all day anyway. Nothing will be different. In return, we get to stay here for our last two years as minors. We will leave on our eighteenth birthday, and you will give us both $500 apiece and never hear from us again," I stated in a convincing tone.

"Are you nuts? That will never work. She will tell

the first moment she gets," Dawn said with frustration.

"She doesn't have a choice. No one is going to take care of her. She is probably paralyzed. If she goes into a home, she won't get anything she loves, like her cigarettes and booze. At least this way, she can stay in the comfortability of her home," I said as I handed Sheryl a cigarette. I took a lighter out of my back pocket and lit it for her. She quickly grabbed the cigarette and took a deep inhale. The smoke made the urine smell worse.

"Damien, she's evil, and you know it. She will happily tell, and we will be going to Juve," Dawn said, shaking her head.

"Sheryl, look at me. You do know I have special powers, right? It's the power that made you mute," I lied. "I can do far worse things than that. This is your only choice. I will even consider giving you back your voice," I lied again. Knowing I didn't have a clue of what happened to her voice.

"Do you agree, Sheryl? Just nod your head if you do," Dawn demanded. Sheryl nodded yes.

"Ok, great!" I expressed as I clapped my hands.

"Okay, Damien. I will go along with this. Who is going to give her a bath?" Dawn asked with her fingers pinching her nose.

We found some scissors and gloves in the kitchen

drawer. We cut Aunt Sheryl out of the clothes she had worn for the past three weeks. It was awful. We grabbed a trash bag and threw the clothes in the bag. We rolled her to the side and removed the feces off her ass and back with the baby wipes. Her hair was matted and smelled pissy from my urine. I decided to cut it. I chopped it off as I had done to Dawn's hair years ago. I smiled at the memory of seeing Dawn with her butchered hair which had fully grown back. After cutting Sheryl's hair, we needed a break before lifting her to bathe her. Luckily there was a full bathroom on the first floor. My grandparents had that side of the house renovated before they passed away. I lit her another cigarette as she laid there on her side naked.

Dawn put a sheet on top of the wheelchair so it wouldn't get dirty. We lifted Sheryl's big ass and put her in the chair. She had actually lost some weight from barely eating on the floor. She was still heavy and overweight. Dawn was annoyed, and she felt she shouldn't have to help. I constantly reminded her of Juve, and she complied. Sheryl's legs didn't seem broken, or maybe she was immune to the pain. We rolled her to the shower and barely got her on the shower seat.

"Dawn, you wash her, and I will go clean up the shit and urine off the floor," I demanded.

"No! You wash her. This was your brilliant idea,"

Dawn yelled.

"Just do it. The next time she can do it herself," I said as I slammed the bathroom door behind me.

I cleaned up all her crap from the floor and mopped the entire downstairs with bleach and pine sol. We dressed her, fed her, and sat her in front of the television. I told her we could call an ambulance to get her legs checked out. She wrote on a paper that she was okay. I knew I had built her trust. We had a few fights over the next two years, and I found myself slapping her here and there. It was a very destructive relationship.

Her once-a-month man cut her off after seeing her chopped hair and the wheelchair. I guess he finally said fuck the money. We moved out at the age of eighteen, as agreed. She gave us $500 apiece as agreed. She asked could we go to the market for her once a month and get her cigarettes and booze. We said we would, but we both knew we would never return. We kept our word about everything else, except giving her back her voice. I think she was better off being quiet anyway. She could keep that damn trapper of hers shut.

11

HE'S BACK

"Damien, Damien! Do you hear me? Help. Please help me," a girl pleaded with her back turned to me.

"I can't see you. What do you need help with? Stop calling my name," I replied.

"But I need you, Damien. Only you can save me. Only you. Only you."

"Turn around so I can help you. Just move slow," I instructed the girl.

"I'm glad you can help. Now start by telling everyone what you did to me," Mr. Ralph said as he turned around to face me, still dressed like a little girl.

I jumped up. Dawn and I were twenty-three years old now. We had been through a lot. I hadn't had a Mr. Ralph nightmare in years and was shocked to see his ugly face popping up in my dreams. I was spending the weekend at Dawn's place so we could try to find our mother. Mama had left years ago and still hadn't returned. We knew she was alive because she sent us postcards with a lousy $50 bill every month. She stopped sending them about two months ago, which alarmed us. Mama had stopped all contact, and that wasn't like her. Although, we hadn't known who Mama had become after she left.

After leaving Aunt Sheryl's house a few years ago, our lives changed drastically. Dawn moved in with our Aunt Lily on Papa's side until she got a good job and moved in with her boyfriend Craig last year. Craig is tall, handsome with a muscular body. He has exceptionally straight teeth, and his dark complexion is smooth. Not dry, but smooth. Dawn and Craig started dating when Dawn turned 20. She met him at her birthday party. I barely received an invitation to Dawn's party. She claimed she thought I would want to do my own thing on our birthday. We had outgrown the twin stuff.

Dawn changed a lot and often acted like I was a burden to her now busy life. She had grown into a stunning young lady. Dawn was always attractive but a little unflattering as a kid. She wasn't developed when we were younger. She was built like a little boy. Her face was beautiful, but she still had to go through that awkward growing-up stage, where your teeth are bigger than your mouth.

Now, Dawn was a slimmer version of Mama. She had a nice amount of curves to fit her 130-pound body. Her face was drop-dead gorgeous. It was hard not to stare at her milky brown flawless skin. Her full pink lips sat perfectly between her defined nose, and long untamed hair fell loosely on her back. Usually, Dawn was a workout freak, and her body reflected all her hard work. However, she seemed to have been slacking in the gym. This time she looked a little chubby.

My life after Aunt Sheryl's wasn't so sweet. I lived in a motel for two weeks until the $500 Aunt Sheryl gave me ran out. I slept on the street many nights, and when it got freezing cold, I had no choice but to knock on Aunt Sheryl's door. She let me sleep in the basement a few times, which sometimes felt colder than outside.

Aunt Sheryl always reminded me to get out the next day by leaving a nice friendly note at the top of the basement steps. She stopped letting me in the last time when I refused to go into the basement. Knowing she couldn't chase me around the house. She was out of the wheelchair, but she walked really slow. I slept where I wanted. I stayed there for three weeks, and she never let me in again. I met a few friends over the years who would let me crash at their places from time to time.

No one taught me about getting a job or anything about being an adult. I was just left alone to figure it out. Dawn often ignored my calls. She's only so welcoming now because I have a job and my own place. She knows I won't need her money or to stay on the floor at her place. Her boyfriend Craig was scheduled to be gone for the weekend on a business trip, but, apparently, it got canceled because he's right with us being the third wheel.

"So, Damien, are you dating anyone?" Dawn asked while pouring us cups of orange juice.

"Not right now. I just got my shit together, you know. I've been focused, for real," I answered while picking up the cup.

"Yeah, I'm glad you got a job and a place. I'm proud of you, twin. Where do you think Mama is now?" Dawn asked.

"So you are not seeing anyone?" Craig asked.

"Craig, don't start. Mind your business," Dawn jumped in.

"What, Dawn? I just find it strange that he never has anyone. All the years I've known you both, I never saw him with anyone," Craig stated as he lifted weights in the dining room.

"All the years I've known you, you have been in my

fucking business. I find that strange," I responded, taking another sip of the orange juice.

"Okay! Can everyone put their dicks back in their pants, please," Dawn yelled with irritation.

"I thought he wasn't going to be here this weekend. Anyway, back to Mama. That is why I'm here, right?" I asked, looking at Dawn.

"Yes, back to Mama. I last heard she was living in Baltimore," Dawn replied.

"Baltimore? Who the hell she knows there? I'm finally caught up on all my bills, so I was thinking of hiring a private investigator."

"I don't think we need one. We can do most things online these days. Save your money," Dawn said.

"Yeah, save your money so you won't have to be asking us for shit," Craig mumbled.

"That's it! I'm sick of your ass. Would you like to say what your real problem is, Bro? Stand up! Get that shit off your chest," I said, standing up.

"Sit down, Damien. You squaring up like you are on the street. That's my fiance. We don't do that in here," Dawn firmly said.

"Fiance? When did you get engaged?" I asked with a confused facial expression.

"I was going to tell you this weekend," Dawn replied.

"This has gone too far, Craig," I responded to

Craig.

"What you mean too far. Am I not worthy of being his wife? Or are you jealous because my life is going good?" Dawn screamed with emotion.

"Jealous, for what? We are equal. Actually, before we both say something, we will regret, I'm leaving. I will see you next week. We can talk about finding Mama over the phone," I said as I started gathering my things.

"Yes, I think that's best," Dawn stated as she helped me gather my things.

I caught the elevator down to the garage. Soon as I opened the door to go to my car, I felt a powerful hard punch to my left eye. It instantly knocked me to the ground. I grabbed the gravel in the dirt to get up, and before I could stand, I felt a kick to the gut, then another one. I flipped over to my back, and before I could fully see who was brutally pounding me, another punch landed on my side temple, and I was blacking in and out. I fought back but felt like I was only swinging in the air. The person was now dragging me, and I could feel my back scraping against the hard concrete. I was kicking and swinging. I finally heard the familiar voice, and I couldn't believe it.

"This is an ass whooping I've been waiting to give you for a long time," Papa said as he stomped my face to the ground."

"Papa, stop. Stop. I'm your son," I weakly mumbled.

"My son? My son? Would a son frame his father for murder?" Papa asked as he punched me in the jaw repeatedly.

"Stop, Stop! Let him go, Sir," The security guard yelled.

"Don't tell me what the fuck to do. This is my rotten-ass child. I will kick his ass as I please," Papa yelled as he kicked me in the back

"Dispatch, call the police. We have a domestic," The security guard yelled in the walkie-talkie.

"Here, you can have this piece of shit. I'm not trying to go back to jail for this scum a second time. Damien, I'm not done with you. You hear me, boy?" Papa tossed me to the guard. It was blood in my eyes, and I could barely see.

"What apartment were you in? Let me get you some help," The guard asked.

"Apartment 33, my twin lives there. Please get her," I begged in a weak tone. A few minutes went by before I heard the most comforting voice ever.

"Oh my God, Damien. Who did this to him? Can he walk? What happened?" Dawn asked while holding me. She held me close, kind of how Mama used to.

"It was Papa. Papa did this," I said in a faint sound before I blacked out.

I woke up in a hospital. I panicked, I immediately thought about my job. I worked so hard to get that job. I hadn't missed a day yet, but there was no way I could go to work under these conditions. Dawn, Craig, and my counselor were there to comfort me. Craig apologized for the fight we had earlier that day. Dawn just kept rubbing my arms and telling me it would be okay. I believed her.

The nurse said I couldn't get a mirror until the day before my release. I guess I wouldn't be too pleased with my new face. My body felt like everything was broken. I had two fractured ribs, multiple bruises, and had suffered head trauma from numerous blows to the head. Everyone left after a few hours. I got an unexpected visitor the next day.

"Hello, Damien. It's been a long time," Detective Ross said with a smile on his face.

"What are you doing here?" I asked in an annoyed tone.

"Who beat you up like that? Wow, you look pretty bad. Maybe, I can help. I am an officer of the law. Do you want to tell me?" Detective Ross asked.

"It was my no-good father. What is he doing out anyway?" I asked in a frustrated tone.

"Oh, I'm sorry, I didn't hear you. I can't discuss family issues," he said with a smirk. "Did you know that your father was sleeping with your neighbor, Miss

Clarisse? You know the one with the big breasts?" Detective Ross asked.

"Yeah, I know her. Papa was a whore, so what?" I asked.

"Well, the funny thing is, your Papa was screwing Clarisse when Mr. Ralph was murdered. So, he did leave out that night. He lied to protect your mother's feelings. Clarisse admitted she was with your father, and he was deemed innocent during his second trial. Dawn didn't tell you?"

"Dawn knew Papa had a second trial?" I asked.

"Yes, she came every day for support. The issue we have now is how your story hasn't been adding up, Mr. Damien. We now have reason to believe you were involved in Ralph Jones's murder," Detective Ross said as he took a seat next to my hospital bed.

"You have reason to be wrong. You don't have anything better to do than to be chasing a ten-year-old case?"

"You lied, Damien. You probably didn't know I visited your father a few times in jail, and it didn't take long to realize you framed him. Why did you do it?" he asked while sipping his coffee.

"I didn't do anything. If I'm not under arrest, I would like for you to leave," I demanded.

"Funny, you should bring up being under arrest. The next time I see you, I will have a pair of my brand new shiny handcuffs. Are you at least curious about how you became a suspect?"

"No! I am curious to know why you are wearing the same suit from the day I met you? Why are you chasing the same old case? You didn't move far in the task force, huh? You are still the same, "don't know shit," detective you were back then," I laughed.

"I always could appreciate a good laugh, Damien. You fucked up by burning down Ralph's house. You really fucked up by messing with Brianna, but most importantly, you fucked up by lying. Me and my cuffs will see you soon," Detective Ross laughed as he left the room.

I was released from the hospital three days later. Papa had been calling my cell phone, threatening me every day. I had already planned on getting a gun and blowing his fucking head off. I was upset with Dawn for not telling me he was getting out. I know she always loved Papa, but she had to know he would be upset.

Papa must've been working out in the jail. His arms were buff, and he was in better shape than most men my age. He looked handsome, and he completely lost the drunk look. I wondered if he knew where Mama was. Detective Ross's slinky ass was becoming a problem as well. Instead of hiring an investigator to find Mama, I probably should be hiring a lawyer.

One question I kept asking myself was, *how did Papa know I was at Dawn's apartment. Did he follow me there? Did he see me come in? Maybe he knew my car.* I decided to quit my job before they fired me. My face was starting to heal, and I needed some money fast. I knew Craig's family had money, and Dawn always bragged about how they kept at least twenty thousand in the house. But I can't steal. I do a lot of shit, but stealing has always been off the radar. I decided to sit in the hospital lobby in a wheelchair and call Dawn. Before I could fully dial the number, I received a call from another blocked number.

"Hello," I answered.

"Hello, Damien. Don't hang up!" Papa demanded.

"What do you want? You already broke my nose and fucked my body up," I yelled.

"I want you to know before Ralph died, he told me something," Papa said.

"I don't care!" I screamed, forgetting I was in the hospital lobby until I saw everyone looking at me.

"When he came over for dinner that night, he told me your secret. I knew all these years, and I never told a soul. Not even when you got me arrested. Exposing you would do more harm to me. I was so disgusted with you. I just wanted you to know, you stopped being my son that night. You are a sinner. So, even if you hadn't framed me, I was never going to be your father again. See you soon, Danny Boy," Papa said before hanging up in my ear. Something about the way he called me Danny Boy made my skin crawl. Mr. Ralph was a lousy sack of shit. Thanks to Papa, I now know I can't go home. I should be safe at Dawn's house because Papa always listens to his precious Dawn. Papa was acting obsessed. My mind was racing, and I knew I would need to leave town soon, but I had one more thing to do before I could go forever.

"Hi, Dawn. Do you think I can crash at your place for two or three days while my body finishes healing?" I asked Dawn on the phone.

"Sure, Damien. I also told Papa he is not allowed around here. He went too far. He could've killed you. Craig is okay with you coming here. He was worried about you too."

"I must've really got my ass whipped for Craig to worry," I laughed.

"Boy, you are so silly. I know, I was shocked. Craig asked about you every day. He even went to see you one day by himself," Dawn giggled.

"Wow! I'm already discharged. They just rolled me to the lobby. I'll be here waiting for you."

"Okay, I'll be there soon. And, oh yeah, I love you, Danny Boy," Dawn replied.

12

THE TRUTH

I stayed at Dawn's house for a week. We all decided to go on a ski trip to get away from everything. It was Dawn's idea. I knew I was leaving the city soon, and it was a few things I wanted to tell Dawn. A lot happened over the years, and there were also many things I kept quiet about. The ski trip was the perfect time to let everything go. I knew after this trip things would never be the same between us, and I was building up the courage to face my secret.

Dawn and Craig were packing. I was in the mirror brushing my waves and caring for my face like I usually do. I brushed my teeth twice, and the idea of going to jail in a dirty cell almost made me vomit. Some of Dawn's other friends were supposed to meet us at the cabin, but they said they would be a day or two behind. I never went skiing before, and I wasn't excited to be breaking any new bones that Papa hadn't already broken. I wondered if this trip was a setup to kill me. Maybe Papa would be waiting at the cabin with a gun. Dawn was being too nice.

I realized I had been in the bathroom for a while. I looked deep in the mirror. My pupils were enlarged. I looked inside my eyes, and for the first time ever, I saw the truth. I saw who I really was, and I saw who I could no longer be. I could no longer be the lie that hid behind my eyes. I looked deeper, and everything flashed before me. It was time to become the real me. I couldn't believe I had let this secret enslave me.

"Damien! Come on! You still take forever in the bathroom. Your teeth are white enough. Let's go!" Dawn demanded, snapping me out of my deep thoughts.

"Girl, you sound like Mama. I'm coming now," I yelled back to the living room. "Here, we go," I mumbled under my breath.

It took two hours to get to the cabin. I was sure to drive my own car, so I would have a way out if need be. I was highly paranoid. Something in my gut just didn't feel right. I didn't know if it was because I was finally telling the truth or something else. The cabin was beautiful. The walls were made of all brick. The fireplace sat back with a deer's head overtop of it. It had six bedrooms, wood floors, and a balcony off each of the upstairs rooms. Craig booked the cabin, it was modernized, yet it still gave you the old wood cabin feel. I knew it was expensive to book for a week. I picked a room and put my stuff in there. After settling, we sat around the fireplace and talked about old times.

"Damien, Papa, really did a number on you, didn't he?" Dawn joked.

"Fuck you, Dawn. That's your damn father. He called me the day when I left the hospital just to tell me I wasn't his son," I said.

"What exactly did you do to him?" Craig asked.

"It's a long story!" Dawn and I answered at the same time.

"Twinsies!" We yelled.

"Dag, we haven't done twinsies since we were living with Sheryl. Have you heard from her?" Dawn asked.

"Nope. Maybe she died by now," I laughed.

"What? That's not funny, Damien. Isn't that your aunt?" Craig asked.

"Well, she used to be our aunt, but then we all decided she would just be Sheryl," Dawn explained.

"Babe, your family is strange. No offense, but y'all weird," Craig said as he kissed Dawn's cheek.

"No offense taken. We own our crazy," I admitted.

"It's been a long night. I'm about to take a shower

and lay down. Babe, come to bed whenever. You know how to wake me up," Dawn gave Craig a dirty smirk.

"Okay, I'll be up. I'll have a few more of these drinks and catch up with Damien, man to man."

"Thank God. Y'all are finally having a mature talk. Good night Damien," Dawn smiled as she headed up the creaky cabin steps.

"I know things have been crazy between us lately," Craig started to talk in a low tone after Dawn shut the bedroom door.

"Crazy? Why are you marrying my sister?" I whispered.

"Damn, straight to it, huh? Damien, this was your stupid idea, and now I actually love her, and you are upset?" Craig whispered.

"Well, I never said marry her. You are in love with me, right?" I asked, looking into Craig's eyes.

"Yes, Damien. I've always been in love with you, which is why I went along with this dumb shit in the first place," Craig said, grabbing my arm.

"Get off of me. You haven't touched me in weeks. The plan was for you to date Dawn and get her to open up to you about some things I was suspicious of. The plan was also so you and I could be together in secrecy as long as Dawn was our cover-up. But you fucked that up," I said, moving back.

"It's not my fault she doesn't tell me shit. She never talks about her past. Why would you make me date your sister anyway? Instead of you just coming out with your big secret of being gay?" Craig asked, grabbing me closer.

"My family would never accept a gay. I had two gay family members they threw away like garbage, and Dawn also hates gays. She would never accept that side of me. But, look at my life now. I did all this to hide my sexuality, and now I'm being accused of murder," I said, raising my voice a little.

"Bring it down. You don't want Dawn to hear you. Murder? Who do they think you murdered?"

"Never mind that the point is the guy that died told my father years ago that I was gay and nothing was going to fix my family anyway. I've been hiding in this closet all this time; meanwhile, I screwed my life up in the process. Now the man I love is marrying my sister," I whimpered as tears filled my eyes. I hadn't cried in years, and it felt good letting out my balled-up emotions.

"Don't cry. I hate to see you cry. What's the game plan? I have to be honest, I love Dawn now. You two are weirdly identical, and I feel like I'm with you when I'm with her. She's an easier version, though. I don't have to tell my family that I'm gay, and my father will continue to support me. He told me the other day he wants to leave the company to me. I will lose everything coming out with this secret," Craig said, grabbing my hand with his strong muscular hands.

"You were the one telling me I should be true to myself, and now you are being a coward?" I barked.

"That was years ago. I was ready to live a life with you, Damien, in the open, but you set this up, and now I know how great life can be if I stay in the closet. This is really your fault. I was so in love with you. I would've done anything you told me to do," Craig confessed.

"Well, I'm telling my truth. I'm tired of carrying this burden around. My father knows now, anyway. There's no way I'm letting you marry my twin. If she still wants to marry you after knowing my dick be in your mouth, then you deserve each other."

"Damien, you are being unfair. Wait, let's talk about this. You are going to hurt so many people."

"Apparently, that's what I do. I hurt people. Good night Craig," I proceeded to walk up the steps.

"Wait," he lowly pleaded.

"Wait for what? I'm done."

"I'm Brandon!" Craig stated.

All night I tossed and turned. I couldn't believe Craig was that mysterious little boy I had played with and looked for after his disappearance. I had so many questions. It dawned on me that he knew Mr. Ralph.

Actually, he lived with him. I couldn't wait to talk to Craig or Brandon or whatever his name was. I knew it would have to be when Dawn wasn't around. I thought of knocking on the door now, but I knew that could possibly make Dawn suspicious.

The following day was tense. I dreamed of losing my virginity to Brianna, which was always a nightmare. It was one of the worst days of my life, losing my virginity to a girl, knowing I was attracted to boys. It was torture. I didn't know how Craig had sex with Dawn. He said it was the worst part of all. When I purposely sent Craig to meet Dawn at her birthday party. I never expected things to go this far or to last this long.

I dreaded spending the next few days with Dawn and Craig together, kissing and loving each other. Craig never had sex with Dawn when I was around. At least I didn't have to hear that shit. Well, I decided today was the day to let the cat out of the bag, whatever that means. I always heard Mama say it. I knew I would no longer have a relationship with Dawn, and Craig would be left to choose who he wanted to be with. Although, I was pretty sure Dawn wouldn't want him anymore.

"So, how did the talk go last night? Did you boys make up?" Dawn asked.

"I apologized to Damien for always dogging him. I

think now, we can move forward," Craig quickly lied. I turned my head and remained silent.

"Ok, let's get in our ski gear. Are you excited, Dawn?" I asked.

"Hell no! I like activities on the ground, but we said we would try new things this year, right, Babe?" Dawn asked Craig.

"Right," he replied.

"Well, it's going to take me a while to get ready. I want to drink a cup of coffee and put on some makeup before we go. Why don't you two go chop us some more wood for tonight, so I don't have to rush," Dawn suggested.

"Ok, Babe, take your time. I made your coffee already. Here my love, and you know you don't need any makeup," Craig flirted.

"Is there a chopping knife already there?" I asked, insinuating that I would chop Craig up if he didn't stop being extra.

"I'm sure it is," Craig awkwardly laughed as he stood tall with his broad shoulders. We walked up the mountain to chop the wood. I walked behind Craig and admired his backside as he aggressively hiked up the mountain.

"Have you lost your fucking mind? Now I think you are just being disrespectful." I said to Craig.

"I'm sorry. I can't just act weird to Dawn. That

would be suspicious."

"Fuck all of that. What did you mean you were Brandon? It's no way," I said, looking into his eyes.

"I am. I wanted to tell you forever. Things got crazy with Dawn, and I was embarrassed to say I was that kid."

"Well, how do you know Ralph? Was he your uncle?" I asked.

"No. I don't want to talk about it," Craig said, turning his face away.

"Craig, you know I would never judge you. How could I? My mother left me with her evil sister, my father is a violent criminal who just whipped my ass, and my twin sister is fucking my lover. You can tell me anything," I confessed.

"Ralph is actually my biological father. My rich parents adopted me after..." Craig stopped talking.

"After what?"

"Do you remember that one day we were playing behind your house and we kissed? It was my first time knowing for sure I like boys. Do you remember?"

"Of course, I remember. You were the first boy I ever liked in that way, but we were only eight, so I wasn't sure I was gay. I was confused. Why did you bring that up?" I asked.

"My real father, Ralph. He saw us. He beat me to a pulp and molested me that night. He said if I wanted a penis, I wouldn't want one again after having his. It was the worst day of my life."

"Oh my God, Craig. You didn't deserve that. You were so kind as a child. I thought you hated me from the kiss, and every time I went looking for you, he said it was never a boy living there. So where did you go after?"

"He kept me tied in the basement for, I guess, a few months until one day he stayed out, and I escaped. I ran to the supermarket where a store clerk called the police. I pretended I didn't know who my parents were, and they put me in foster care, where the Smiths eventually adopted me. I was nine."

"I always saw something familiar in your eyes from the very first day I met you. Now I know what it was. I love you, Craig, and I'm so sorry that happened to you," I said as I grabbed his chest closer to mines.

"I love you too! But there's one more thing I have to tell you," Craig said.

"No, you don't! You don't have to tell me anything else. That is all in the past. Let's just focus on Dawn and get through the day. I hate that he did that to you. Now I know how he knew my secret. I could never figure it out."

"But, I do think I should tell you this one last thing," Craig tried to explain. Before he could say another word, I grabbed him and slammed him in the snow, and started kissing him.

"Shut up," I said in a seductive voice. Craig shut up, and we passionately made love on the snow. It was freezing, but our body heat kept us warm. We started getting dressed, and I turned around. I could feel the stare of a hulk on my neck.

"What the fuck! You are gay?" Dawn screamed at me first instead of Craig.

"Dawn, wait. Calm down," Craig said as he pulled up his pants.

"Calm down. Bitch, you were just fucking my twin brother. You fucking booty-loving whores," Dawn yelled, charging towards Craig.

"Dawn, I wanted to tell you, and I had planned on telling you during this trip," I explained.

"Shut up! You always wanted everything I had. You are a fucking disgrace, "Dawn said to me.

"I never wanted to hurt you, Dawn," Craig interrupted.

"The wedding is off. I would never marry you. As a matter of fact, you can leave before I take this knife and shove it up your sweet ass. This is between me and my sister," Dawn sarcastically said, calling me her sister instead of her brother.

"Wait, Baby. We can…" Craig tried to explain as Dawn threw a brick at his head.

"Baby? I'm not your fucking Baby, but I am

carrying your baby. Did you tell your little boyfriend that?" Dawn quizzed as she looked for something else to grab.

"You got her pregnant? Are you fucking serious?" I asked Craig.

"Damien, I tried to tell you. I never wanted all this to happen. This is mainly your fault. Did you tell Dawn what you did while you are pointing fingers?" Craig asked.

"Just leave Craig. I can't discuss this with you right now," I said to intervene before he said too much.

"Tell me what? Huh, Damien. What else did you do to me?" Dawn questioned, walking closer to me.

"Calm down, Dawn. Think about the baby. We can all fix this," Craig insisted.

"Bitch! There is nothing to fix. You will never see this baby, and that's if I keep it," Dawn implied.

"If you think I won't see my child, you are crazy. You know what, I'm out of here. Damien, never mind, just never mind," Craig said as he rushed down the mountain. A few minutes later, we heard Craig's car screeching off.

"Ok, Damien. It's just you and me now. Let's get this shit out because, after today, I will never talk to you again. You are officially dead to me."

"Dawn, do you know what I've been through just to hide this from everyone? I've done unimaginable things," I confessed.

"I don't give a fuck! How long have you been fucking my man?" Dawn asked as she picked up the chopper knife.

"He's not your man and put the knife down. We can really talk and get this shit out in the open. I have questions, like how did Papa know I was at your house?" I asked.

"Boy, fuck your questions. I have questions too, like what the hell happened to Brianna?" Dawn yelled as she charged me with the chopping knife.

"Dawn, put the knife down! We are on top of a mountain. I didn't do anything to Brianna but regrettably, fuck her. Ain't no dick worth either of us dying," I pleaded as I moved back.

"You are already dead to me," she said as she swung the knife at me again.

"Dawn, stop!" I begged as she succeeded in her first slice on my arm. I watched the blood leak as I leaned back. Everything became still. All of a sudden, the commotion was over. I no longer heard Dawn's voice. I heard nothing but the wind blowing at the top of the mountain. Dawn was gone.

Before I knew what was happening, I had pushed Dawn off the mountain. Dawn didn't fall all the way to the bottom. She fell about ten feet and landed on a rock. I saw blood coming from her head. Against my better judgment, I decided to leave her. She was bitter and angry and would definitely send me to jail. It was the hardest thing I ever had to do. I loved Dawn, but I didn't trust her. It was why I wanted Craig to get some information out of her. It wasn't until I got away from Dawn that I started feeling differently. I contemplated over and over again going down the mountain to help her. I decided not.

I had to speed back to Dawn's apartment to get my things and the money Craig put up for me to skip town. He told me while we were having sex, he would come with me wherever I went. It was a horrible ride back to the city as my mind raced. I didn't want to kill Dawn. I knew not having her alive would destroy a piece of me too. I sadly left that piece of me bleeding to death on a mountain. I figured I would surely go to jail now if I was caught.

The entire ride, I couldn't get Craig off my mind. I wondered how things got so messy. I regretted stopping him from telling me about the baby. I could've been more prepared to handle the situation. Damn, if I killed Dawn, then I killed my niece or nephew. This is just too much to think about. Not to mention Detective Ross is all over my ass. My emotions were all over the place. I wondered what happened to Craig's real mother, and if Ralph was his father, why wasn't he enrolled in school with the rest of us. Why did Ralph try to hide his own child? I wondered whether he abused Craig sexually prior to him seeing us kiss.

My thoughts are back on Dawn. I hope she is okay. I'm feeling an emotion I've never really felt, and that's guilt. I feel guilty for everything. I regret setting Dawn and Craig up in the first place. Even if Dawn is okay, she will never forgive me. I allowed her to sleep with my gay lover, and I threw her off a cliff. My only thoughts now are skipping town and trying to forget everything. I really missed Mama. I missed her beautiful face and her loud mouth. No matter what I did, she never denied me. She will have to disown me if it comes out I killed Dawn. I wonder whether she would accept me being gay; she kind of accepted the idea of me being a murderer. Mama never lost complete contact with us. I prayed she was okay. My thoughts were overwhelming, and I couldn't control the anxiety feeling that overtook me.

I got back to Dawn's place in one hour and twenty minutes. I did 100 the entire drive until I reached the city limits. I trashed her place, looking for the money. It wasn't where Craig said it was, and his phone was going straight to his voicemail. After much searching. I only found a lousy $300 and a few of Dawn's diamonds. I was running out of time. I took the money and whatever else I could.

I looked around Dawn's place, which looked so much like her. It was all her favorite things, and I saw very little of Craig's belongings except his workout equipment. I found myself slowing down and mourning Dawn. I played with all her stuff and smelled her jacket she had on the day before. I admired a picture she took the day we left Sheryl's. It took me right back to those periods of us sticking together. I laughed at us torturing Sheryl and her always drinking the last of the milk just to annoy me.

I thought of the story Mama told me about Dawn grabbing my hand when we were babies. I've killed the only person who truly loved me. Craig loves me, but Dawn loves me like no other. I jumped out of my thought and put Dawn's jacket down. I looked at the apartment just one more time, and I said to myself, "goodbye, twin." I jumped out of my thoughts and remembered that time was of the essence. I opened the front door.

"Mr. Damien Scott, we are arresting you for the murder of Ralph Jones and the disappearance of Brianna Scottsdale. You have the right to remain silent. Anything you say can and will be used against you in a court of law. Do you understand these rights?" Detective Ross said with a grin. I remained silent.

My heart instantly fell in my chest. Fear had taken

over my body as I could hear each heartbeat thump louder and louder. My gut felt sick, almost like I could vomit. My feet felt stuck as if I couldn't move as the cops slapped a pair of cold metal cuffs on my fragile wrists. I thought of life in prison as a gay man and decided to continue being straight. It could only help where I was going. I thought of Mama and got an uneasy feeling as another cop slammed me against Dawn's door.

When I got outside, I saw Papa standing across the street smoking a cigar with a devilish look on his face. He took great pleasure in watching me get thrown in the back of the police car. He looked me dead in my eyes and walked away. I lowered my head as I knew my luck had run out. Suddenly, I fainted. I could only assume the stress took over my body. I woke up in front of the same prison I had sent Papa to years ago. All I could think of was Dawn. Something didn't feel right. My thoughts were interrupted by an obnoxiously loud voice.

"Welcome home, Boys. Shut up, take off all your belongings, put them in the brown paper bag to your right. Be prepared to get fully undressed and bend over," The tall, thick white correctional officer screamed.

13

NIGHTMARES

Oh, my head is killing me. The thumping is overwhelming. My sight is fading. Is that blood? Where am I? Shit, can I move? Oh my God, my leg is not moving. HELP!!!!! Is anyone here? Help!!! I dragged my legs across the rock as blood poured from my head. I felt discombobulated. I can't remember how I got here. I heard a group of what sounded like my friends walking above me, laughing, playing, and joking.

"Help! Please Help!" I screamed in a weak, faint sound. For a split second, all I heard was silence.

"Yo, Bro, I think someone is down there. Did you hear that?" My friend Mark asked.

"Nah, man, you letting them shrooms get to you.

You hearing shit," another guy answered with laughter.

"Please help! I'm down here!" I screamed louder.

"Oh my God, someone is down their assholes. It sounds like a woman," my friend Vanessa stated.

"Oh, shit. It's Dawn," Mark yelled.

I blacked out. I woke up seven days later in a hospital with an IV stuck in my arm. I had white bandages around my head and my knee cap. I felt my head and a cool sensation on my scalp as I realized I was shaved bald. I heard beeping noises from multiple machines. I blinked my eyes slowly. They felt so heavy. Flashes of what happened to me started appearing in my mind as clear as a perfect glass of water. I saw Damien pushing me over the mountain, and I jumped. I heard the nurse calling the doctor.

"Well, look who is finally awake. How do you feel?" asked the old heavy doctor with a thick mustache whose name tag read Dr. Smidget.

"Where am I? I feel confused," I confessed.

"You are at Sainte Union Hospital, and you were brought to us with a brain trauma. Do you remember anything that happened to you?" Dr. Smidget asked, moving a flashlight back and forth across my eyes.

"No, I don't remember anything," I lied.

"I was afraid of this. Dawn, I'll be honest with you. I believe you have acute amnesia. We were hoping your memory wouldn't be lost from the incident. It seems you might have been on a ski trip, and you fell. What we couldn't figure out is why would you go skiing alone?"

"I'm not sure. I'm not sure of anything. I can't remember if I even knew how to ski. Did any family come looking for me? Did I get a visit?"

"Uhm, I think we'll let the cops talk to you about that later. For now, I just have a few basic questions before I let you rest up," Dr. Smidget stated in a nervous tone.

"Why did you tense up when I mentioned family? Do I have a family?" I questioned.

"Dawn, everyone has a family of some kind. Let's get to these questions, so you get some rest. Please tell me your full name, age, your biological parents' names, and any siblings."

"I'm assuming my name is Dawn, although I only remember screaming, "Help!" and now I'm here. I don't know my parents' names, but I feel confident I have no siblings. I kind of feel like an only child, or maybe I'm adopted. From the look of my hands, I'm assuming I'm in my twenties. I don't know for sure, though," I falsely stated in a soft, compassionate voice.

"So you're telling me you don't remember your parent's name or the fact that you are a twin?" the doctor asked, hitting my knees for the reflection test.

"A twin? Uhhh, this is too much. I think I would know if I was a twin. Dr. Smidget, is it? This is making no sense."

"I know. But with all this bad news, I do have some good news. The baby is okay. It's like a miracle for a fetus to survive under such traumatizing conditions. Your heartbeat was so faint, it's hard to believe either of you survived.

"A baby? I'm pregnant? I asked as I looked down at the ring on my finger. "Were you able to reach my husband or someone?" I asked in a curious tone. I was hoping they didn't tell Craig anything about me.

"No, I'm sorry. We called your fiancé multiple times, but unfortunately, his phone kept going to voicemail. Your friends who brought you to the hospital said he should've been with you. We informed the police in case he needed help out in the mountains," Dr. Smidget said in a sympathetic tone.

"So, I'm pregnant, engaged, and I have a twin. But I can't remember anything," I said in a frustrating tone.

"Ok, Dawn, that's enough for today. I will call your friends and let them know you woke up today. They will be pleased. We must monitor you and the little one for the next few days. Please let us know if you remember anything. The staff is happy to help. We were all rooting for you and your baby's speedy recovery," the doctor stated as he wrote, "WELCOME BACK" on the board before leaving the hospital room.

Soon as the doctor left, my thoughts immediately went to Damien. He has severely underestimated the power of little oh Danny Girl. Damien was so incompetent to think I was quiet and innocent all these years. He actually thought I didn't feel him cutting all my fucking hair off when we were thirteen or the fact that he hid the milk in the fridge just to try to torture me. Oh, and who the hell did Damien think made Papa have those nightmares that he was always conveniently in. Yeah, he scared Uncle Robby, but I'm the one who took his voice. I had to; he saw me following Papa one day.

Papa was flirting with a woman, and I stared intensely. It made me angry, so I closed my eyes tight and made Papa fall in the street. Everyone thought he was drunk, but Uncle Robby saw the whole thing. At that very moment, Damien walked past and whispered something to Uncle Robby. I silenced him at that precise second.

Poor Uncle Robby never spoke again. I was amazed at how strategic I could be. Uncle Robby's brain was permanently fogged. I was only seven years old, and I didn't know how to use my strength yet. I just didn't want him to tell. I later tried giving him his voice back, but it didn't work that way. What is done is done. I learned that my power was irreversible.

I had no problem taking care of Ralph's ass too. He put his dirty old hands up my skirt one day when Papa wasn't home. He lied and said Papa was right behind him, and I let him in. He happened to have ice cream. I sat next to him on the sofa, licking the ice cream with great pleasure. Mama never bought ice cream, so it was always a treat when someone else gave it to us. Without a word spoken, he slipped his nasty hands up my skirt and took a long slow lick off the ice cream. Instead of screaming, I allowed him to play around under my skirt until he stopped. I can still hear his voice saying, "Next time, we can go a little further, princess." I made my mind up right then and there that it wouldn't be the next time. So, that day he came over to eat dinner with Papa; I decided that would be the last day he would enter my house.

I snuck out of the house after everyone was asleep. I walked to Mr. Ralph's house; along the way, I found a stick with nails sticking out, and I decided it would be perfect. I pretended to be crying as I knocked on Mr. Ralph's door in an obnoxious way. I saw him come to the window and move the curtains to the side. I looked up with tears in my eyes. He slightly smiled with his pink and brown lips. He walked over to answer the door.

"What's wrong, Princess. What are you doing here?" Mr. Ralph asked, standing in the doorway with a wife-beater shirt and oversized boxer briefs. His legs reminded me of sticks. His eyes roamed my entire body as if I was dessert.

"I hate my life! Everyone is so mean to me. Damien is a fucking jerk, my dad is a drunk and Mama is so weak. All I do is try to be a good girl, and they are all so mean. I didn't have anywhere else to go. Can I please come in, Mr. Ralph," I cried.

"Don't cry! Come on in here. I understand. My family gets on my damn nerves too. Why do you have that stick?" he asked, looking at the stick.

"It's late, and I was scared. I carried it for protection in case someone on the street tried to mess with me or something," I said as I wiped the tears from my cheeks.

"Yeah, it is late. You can leave the stick outside now. Does anyone know you are here?" Mr. Ralph asked as he peeked out the doorway.

"No one knows I'm here. I must keep the stick inside, or they will know I'm here. Everyone knows this is the stick from our backyard. It will be a clear giveaway."

"Ok, are you hungry? You can grab some food from the fridge. Your Mama packed me some leftovers from dinner earlier. I was sad it was no ice cream for dessert," Mr. Ralph said with a wink and a dirty look on his face.

"Mama, don't buy ice cream," I bluntly responded.

"I'll keep that in mind. Eat up and then come upstairs and meet me in the bedroom. You can sleep with me so you can feel safe. You can go home in the morning."

I stayed downstairs for about ten minutes, planning how I was going to murder Mr. Ralph. I slowly walked up the steps, and each step creaked. I held the stick in my hand with the nails face outward so I wouldn't poke my leg. I entered his darkroom. He laid there naked, and I almost vomited at the sight of seeing his old wrinkled body. I walked closer to him, and I put the stick outward across the side of the bed. I got on top of him with all my clothes on.

"I know you may not know how this works, but you have to get undressed, Princess. I won't hurt you, and I promise to take it slow. I will only put in a little if you want," Mr. Ralph said as he looked down at his scribbled-up penis.

"I'm not your fucking Princess, and I'm lactose intolerant, so fuck your ice cream. Good night!"

I grabbed the stick from the side of the bed and made sure the first blow was to his head so he couldn't overpower me. I repeatedly struck him until my arms felt weak as I stayed on top of his naked, limp body. It was my first kill. It felt great. I took off Damien's clothes he wore earlier that day and put them in a black plastic bag. I changed into my clothes, walked the black bag to a spot in the field, and buried it. I planned on framing Damien but, he messed that plan up when he framed Papa.

The next morning when Damien woke up, I had planted memories in his mind, and he thought he killed Mr. Ralph. I then started haunting him with nightmares to keep up the momentum. Damien didn't know I could read his mind. Once, I made Mama make him biscuits when Damien was mad at her. He actually thought he was powerful enough to control Mama. I also made Mama go under her bed and pray like a weirdo just to freak Damien out.

Poor Brianna. He made me kill her. If he wouldn't have tried to come between us, she would still be alive. She called me, saying she no longer wanted to be my friend—some bullshit about me being too bossy. Well, I followed her and Damien the night she went missing. I saw him stick his little pinky of a penis in her, and it made me sick to my stomach. I almost spit up behind the bleachers where I hid. He didn't even seem to care about her. He fucked her, and in return, she fucked me over. How dare she stop being my friend just to get screwed by Damien. Oh, it made me so upset. After their disgusting encounter, I followed her down the street. I initially just wanted to confront her, but she made that difficult. I approached her once Damien was far enough away not to see me.

"Brianna!" I yelled.

"What the fuck do you want?" she screamed and jumped with tears coming down her eyes.

"I want to talk to you. Are you crying?" I calmly asked. I initially disregarded her anger towards me.

"Leave me alone! I thought I told you earlier I didn't want to be your friend anymore. I never want to see you or your psycho-sick-ass brother again!" She screamed and walked faster.

"What happened? Just stop and talk to me," I pleaded.

"Talk to you? I never liked you, Dawn. We hung out every day because you showed up every day. I was only your friend in the hopes of getting closer to Damien, which was a huge mistake. When I was younger, I forced myself to be your friend because I was afraid of you. I constantly had these nightmares about you killing me if I didn't be your friend. But now I'm tired of pretending. I hate you and your brother!" Brianna stated, firmly staring intensely into my eyes.

"Brianna, you better choose your words more wisely. I know you are upset about Damien, but I told you not to go! I know you don't mean any of those things you said. How could you fake being someone's friend since elementary school?" I laughed.

"Easy! I did it! Fear, that's how. Well, Dawn, it's time for you to scare someone else because I'm done. I'm also telling everyone in school to stay away from the psycho twins! No one really likes you; they just deal with you because of me. Oh, this feels so good to finally tell you off. Now, get away from me psycho, before I...."

The next thing I knew is I had a string around Brianna's neck. She fought gasping for air, and I enjoyed suffocating her with every ounce of my strength. It wasn't as much pleasure as killing Mr. Ralph, but it was enough to make me feel powerful and to shut her the fuck up. She kicked and punched the air. The more she fought, the stronger I became. I then let her stiff body drop to the ground. I knew I couldn't leave her on the sidewalk strangled to death, although I did consider it would immediately implicate Damien. One sick reason I needed Damien around was to have someone to blame. If he went to jail, I could never use him to take the blame for my dirty work. It made sense to me, although logically, it sounds insane.

So I wrapped my hand around Brianna's long thick hair that I always envied and dragged her to Mr. Ralph's house. Since his death, his house had been vacant, and no one would be going in there anytime soon. The sky was pitch dark, and the nighttime air slowly blew past my face. I could feel the wind blowing the little strings of Brianna's hair that hung loose. The random strings I didn't wrap around my fingers. I quickly dragged her to the back door, so I could get away from the main street. I glanced at my watch, which read 3:07 a.m. I knew it wouldn't be much traffic; however, I could be caught at any given moment. Someone could glance out their window and see me. *How could I explain dragging a dead body?*

I entered Mr. Ralph's freezing cold house, which instantly gave me the chills. I opened the basement door and threw Brianna's body down the steps. Mr. Ralph's face kept flashing in my mind, and I could feel his presence still in the house. I knew I had to think quickly because if I kept Brianna's body in his basement exposed, someone could possibly smell her. I decided to come back in a few days to burn the entire house down before she started rotting away. I felt that would kill both of their memories, and my problems would be solved.

Just one thing fucked this plan up, and it was, oh dear Mama. When I rushed out of Mr. Ralph's house, I saw Mama wandering the streets. She pretended she didn't see me come out of Mr. Ralph's house. I was convinced she hadn't seen me. I had to erase that conclusion when Brianna's death came to light; Mama never looked at me the same. Mama knew I burned the house down, but she never told anyone. I think she convinced herself Damien made me do it. Either way, keeping her mouth shut was the intelligent thing to do. But sometimes, Mama doesn't act too smart.

The worst of it all is the night Aunt Sheryl, or should I say Sheryl came into my room in the middle of the night. She said I was a dirty little slut, and I probably wanted to be a whore like my mother. Sheryl flopped on my bed with a mist of funk following her and asked, what do little whores do? I ignored her and pretended to be asleep. She pulled the covers down and continued to talk. I laid there in a thin nightgown, freezing. The house always had a permanent draft. I can still remember the conversation like yesterday.

"Can I please have the covers back?" I politely asked.

"Why do you want to cover up now? I see how you walk around this house half-naked, flaunting your young body."

"I don't. I just want to go to sleep."

"You are a liar and a whore. I saw you. Since you want to be such a slut. I will treat you like one. Now suck my breast. This doesn't mean I like women or little kids. It just means I'm teaching you a lesson," Sheryl said as she grabbed one long dirty breast from her bra.

"What? No!" I yelled.

"Well, get ready to live in the cold. Today is only twelve degrees. It's a cold one. I will throw your ass right on the street. You can start prostituting. That's what you want anyway.

"No, it's not. I haven't even been with one boy Aunt Sheryl," I confessed.

"Shut the fuck up! My nipples are getting cold. Warm them up, and I'll do the rest. It's not like I want you to suck me off or anything. That would be gay, and I'm no homo," she said with her breast in her hand.

"I have to go to the bathroom first. I had to pee all night. I'll be back," I said in a low, sad tone.

"Hurry up and don't try no slick shit cause I'll put you and Damien's ass out.

I walked past Sheryl slowly, and she smacked my ass. I decided to kill her at that very moment. I first went to the bathroom and shut the door. I knew if I stabbed her, it would be a mess and more complicated to cover up. I also didn't want to be homeless. I flushed the toilet and ran the water as if I was washing my hands. The bathroom was the first room when you came up the steps. I decided to hide on the sidewall.

After a few minutes, I heard Sheryl get up to see what was taking me so long. She slowly peeked in the bathroom. All the lights were out in the house, and I knew Sheryl could barely see because she used her hands to feel the wall to see where she was going. She peeked in Damien's room and then came towards the steps.

I moved back and pushed her down the steps with all my might. It sounded like an earthquake. I knew Damien would wake up, so I immediately switched his dream to something more soothing, to relax him. I went over to Sheryl's body and repeatedly kicked her in her ribs. She could move, and her legs were fine, but she was hurt from the fall. I punched her in her breast over and over again since she wanted to put those nasty things in someone's mouth. I opened her mouth and spat inside. She started screaming, so I muted the Bitch. I pulled her hair so hard and kicked her in the back. After I finished torturing her, I peacefully went to sleep. I heard Damien get up a couple hours later, and I watched him smack her around. I was proud of him for a change. She trembled every time I was near because she knew I was the real monster.

Damien is weak compared to my strength. He really fucked up trying to kill me. Danny boy has a nice treat coming to him. He thinks he liked getting fucked by Craig; wait until I fuck him. His nightmares are the least of his problems. He thought Papa whipped his ass. Who does he think called Papa over there that day to fuck him up? Papa had been waiting for Damien since his release. I talked Papa into waiting until Damien's life was going good before he gave him the beat down.

It killed me to wait. Every time Damien called begging for money, I started to send Papa on his ass. I learned to be patient. It takes great patience to fuck up people's lives. It's the reason I didn't kill Ralph the day he insulted me. I had to wait until a more appropriate time. Papa was out of prison for six months before giving Damien his overdue ass whopping. It was a long hard wait. When I saw Damien beat to a pulp in the garage that day, joy ran through my body. I held him as if I cared for him, while all along, I knew I had set him up. The entire time, I was texting Papa all the details, down to the moment Damien left out of my apartment upset with Craig. Which now, I understand why Craig and Damien always argued.

My first thought when I left the hospital was to find Damien. I quickly found out he had been arrested for all my murders when the news broadcast blasted it across my screen as I lay in the hospital bed. His arrest would seem to be enough punishment for trying to kill me, but it wasn't. I received no satisfaction knowing he was locked up behind bars. I wanted to torture him. I had to.

Also, since I woke up from the hospital, I couldn't

use my power to create nightmares. Maybe I hit my head so hard, and I haven't fully recovered yet, according to the doctors. On the news, it said Damien had a 200,000 cash bond. I've just decided to take the money I stole from Craig's gay ass and get Danny boy released from prison. I knew I shouldn't have trusted a guy named Craig who works out all damn day. Plus, we only had sex twice a month, some bullshit about his training. I was so damn stupid, but I'll take care of Craig's ass too. I can only destroy one person at a time. Right now, it's Damien's time.

When I'm finished with Damien, he will wish he was still behind bars. First, I must keep this amnesia act up. It will work in my favor for everything. My stomach started hurting out of thin air. I felt a sharp pain in my lower abdomen, which was intense. I hit the nurse button, and before long, there was an entire entourage of hospital staff surrounding me. They had to perform an emergency c-section. I was relieved, but I decided to never tell Craig I had lost our baby. I would use it to get him close enough to hurt his ass. It wouldn't be strange for him not to feel my stomach because he knew he could never touch me again after what I witnessed. Yeah, this fake pregnancy thing could work so I could handle his ass.

I was released from the hospital four days later. I was diagnosed with amnesia, sent home with some pills, and told to rest. I wanted to write Damien a letter, but that could incriminate my amnesia story. I decided I would anonymously pay his bail. The day that I got released, I immediately went to the bank. Luckily my friends gave all my belongings to the hospital. I paid a woman I found on the street to go inside the precinct and pay for Damien's bail. I patiently waited for her to come out of the police station. It seemed to have taken forever. I patted her down to ensure she didn't keep the money, and I asked for proof of the posted bail.

Soon as I read the paperwork, I was relieved to see the words, "Bail posted." The woman informed me that the police told her he would not see the bail commissioner until Monday, so he would have to stay in over the weekend. I paid the random street woman, and I caught a cab straight to my apartment, which to my surprise, had been trashed. If I didn't consider killing Damien before, he made my decision easier now, knowing that he trashed my apartment. I decided to deal with Craig later. My entire focus was on Damien. I knew I would need some help pulling off this little amnesia act, so I called Dr. Smidget.

"Hello, Dr. Smidget. This is Dawn. You told me to call you if I could remember anything so you could follow my case. Do you have a minute?" I asked in a calm, subtle voice.

"Of course, Dawn. I'm glad you called. I was actually going to give you a ring because there was a mistake with your tox report, and it seems you had a drug named, Botulinum in your system. This particular drug causes temporary paralysis. I've informed the police," Dr. Smidget stated as he impatiently waited for my response.

"What! I was drugged! This is just too much. Who would do this? Why would someone try to hurt me? I don't understand. I came to this destroyed apartment, and nothing is familiar!" I screamed.

"Calm down, Dawn. I know this is a bit much, but we still have hope you will regain your memory, and maybe all of this will no longer be a mystery. You mentioned you were calling to tell me something? Did you remember something?" Dr. Smidget asked with much anticipation in his voice.

"No! Actually, I still don't remember anything. I'm not even confident my name is Dawn. When I was in the hospital, you said I had a twin. I thought if I had any chance of remembering my old life, seeing my twin could surely help. Who could forget their own twin?"

"Well, I'm not sure if that's an option right now. Damien may not be in a predicament to see you at the moment."

"Well, if I can somehow get him to call you, can

you explain to him my diagnosis, and maybe he will be willing to tell me about our childhood, our parents, or anything. Please, Dr. Smidget, I'm begging you. I can't live, lost like this. I need to know who I am. Please," I begged with a sincere tone.

"Alright, Dawn. My wife's sister is actually a counselor at the jail. I'll see if I can call in a favor. I also think it will help your progress.

"Thank you so much! The sooner, the better! I'm truly losing my mind over here. Thanks again, Doc, for taking care of my brain. I hope to be better soon."

"Sure thing. Don't forget we have a follow-up in two weeks. Oh, one more question, if I can get Damien to agree to speak with you, how would you like him to contact you?"

"Please give him my phone number and address. I won't be going anywhere. Everything is too strange right now," I responded with a convincing tone.

"No problem. Take care, Dawn, and don't forget, I'm just a phone call away," Dr. Smidget stated before hanging up.

Monday came as fast as a blink of an eye. I woke up anticipating my visit from my long-lost twin. I hoped Dr. Smidget got his call through, and I sure hope he could convince Damien about the amnesia. I know Damien well. He has always been curious and will surely want to see if I really forgot everything, and he also likes to think he is so smart. So I'm sure he would surely arrive if he got the message. I started to worry as the day went on; maybe he wouldn't show. Perhaps he was more of a coward than I gave him credit for. Perhaps he would just skip bail and mess up the poor woman credit who bailed him out.

As my thoughts rambled on, time went by fast. It wasn't long before the clock read 11:20 p.m. I gave up and jumped in the shower. As the water ran down my long legs, I felt a sense of disappointment. I felt beaten, and even worse, I felt disturbed because my mental powers still hadn't returned. I had been manipulating people for so long, I had no idea how to be normal.

Suddenly, I heard a knock at the door. The knock was alarming. I couldn't tell if it was the sound of the police knocking, a neighbor informing me of a fire, or someone who had been knocking for a while. Either way, the particular knock grabbed my attention, and it sounded urgent. I turned off the shower and snatched a towel. I slowly walked to the door as the knock got louder and louder. My knees hadn't fully recovered from the fall. Without looking in the peephole, I opened the door.

"Hello, Dawn! Amnesia, huh? Still, up to your old tricks, I see. I know you are surprised to see me."

"What the fuck?" I mumbled.

"When I heard the news, I knew I had to come right away! I've been waiting for this day, far longer than you could ever imagine. What's wrong, Danny girl? You look like you've seen a ghost! You look scared. I know the look of fear. It's a look I had many days with you in my life. I was actually terrified. I had never been so scared in my life as I was that night. Were you expecting someone else? Oh, let me guess, you are waiting for... Damien? Did I get it right? Yup, I got it right. I can tell by the look on your pathetic face. What perfect timing this is! I can't wait to see Damien too. Now sit your Bitch ass down and wonder how you will get out of this. You won't! I have a gun pointed right at your cold heart, and Bitch, it only takes one pop to lay your ass down. Now, how long before Danny Boy gets here?" Brianna asked with a gun pointed at my chest.

I sat in silence as my heart thumped with anxiety. *I couldn't believe Brianna was alive. I knew I set her on fire. How did she survive? Where has she been all these years? She laid there dead for 3 days. How is she alive? How is this happening?* My thoughts were interrupted by a major blow to the head. I started to scream for help, but Brianna was so focused on my every move. She didn't even blink as she waited to smack me with the gun again.

"You look confused. Well, no time to explain. Just know the thoughts you are thinking are some of your last. Oh, I wanted to tell you before our other guest arrives, the nightmares stopped when you thought I was dead. Explain to me how they work?" Brianna asked.

"I'm not explaining shit. I don't know what you are talking about?" I quickly responded.

"Sure, you do! I don't like your tone, so you better be nicer," Brianna said as she hit me in the temple with the gun.

"Okay, okay!" I pleaded with my hands up. I could tell Brianna was serious.

"Now, back to the nightmares. How did you do it, and why did it stop?" she asked while waving the gun around.

"I don't know how? But it started when I was a child. It stopped when I hit my head. I lost the ability to control everyone's dreams. Yours stopped because I thought you were dead. Brianna, I need help," I cried.

"Bitch, please. You need God and don't worry, you'll be meeting him really soon. So, you controlled other people's dreams. I meant nightmares, too?" She asked with a curious facial expression.

"Yes. Just you, Papa, Mama, and Damien. It only worked with people I've been around a lot. I can't just jump into a stranger's dream and turn it into a nightmare. It doesn't work like that. It has to be people

I know on a deeper level. I also can't do it when people are too far away from me unless they are mentally weak," I explained as I whimpered.

"Yeah, you fucked up alright, but that's not my problem. The only thing I need from you now is…." Brianna said, waving the gun around before she was interrupted by a phone call. She didn't answer, nor did she even look to see who was calling. Brianna refused to take her eyes off me. She was smart. She knew the monster I was, and one distraction could cost her life. One slip up, and her ass was mine.

For the first time since Brianna returned, I actually looked at her. She had light burn marks on her left arm and specks of burn marks on her neck. Her face was unharmed and was more gorgeous than ever. Her lashes were long, and she grew into her overdeveloped body. She was shaped like Mama, but her stomach was flatter. Her hips were perfectly formed, and her breast now fit her slim waist. All her teenage features now fit perfectly on her face. Besides the burn marks, Brianna was flawless.

There was a sturdy two hard knocks at the door. Brianna's face lit up like a brand new Christmas tree. I frowned and hoped it was Papa or someone that could help. I looked at Brianna, who stood on the side of the door, solid and firm. She cocked the gun back and put her index finger over her perfectly shaped lips to tell me to be quiet. My heart thumped with anticipation to see who was on the other side of the door. I had never been so scared.

"It's open," Brianna calmly stated. The door opened, and two gunshots were fired. I don't know if I'm dreaming or if I'm dead. I'm in a dark place, and I can't see anything. The sounds are muffled, and I can't seem to find my body parts, but I can still hear my thoughts in my mind. My energy is vital. I'm trying hard to listen. I'm trying hard to hear Brianna, Damien, or anyone for that matter. But I can't. I can only hear my thoughts. I can't picture anyone's face except my own, which is also Damien's. I can't smell, but I feel a warm sensation, and that gives me hope.

Maybe, I'm not dead. Maybe, I'm stuck in a nightmare. I'm trying hard to wiggle my toes, but I can't feel them. I can't even see a reflection of my hand. The warmth I felt seconds ago is gone, and now it feels like a chill. My space is now completely silent. Not even the muffled sounds are here anymore. Where is here? I want to open my eyes, but all I see is darkness. I'm not sure I have eyes anymore.

Damien once told me, "the truth is within the eyes." I want to blink so badly. I want to feel. For the first time ever, I asked God for help. I hate to admit that I'm afraid. I've never felt real fear, and it feels unwelcoming to my body. If I still have a body. I can feel myself leaving wherever I am.

Everything is fading, including my thoughts. I'm fighting for consciousness, but I can feel it drifting away. I'm pretty sure I'm dead now. If I can only blink my eyes, I'll tell the truth about everything. Damien at least deserves the truth before I'm gone forever. Damien's secret is nothing compared to the secret that lives within my death. If the truth is really within the eyes, I can only hope my eyelids will open again. I've now lost my thoughts, and I have nothing left but a blank stare into the deep darkness.

About The Author

Sunni T. Connor is an author from Baltimore, MD, who now resides in California. Her underground Bestseller DAMAGED little girl enhanced her writing career and helped her get recognition as a solid author. Sunni is an impeccable motivational speaker and a serial entrepreneur. She has two beautiful children, amazing parents, and one hell of a soulmate.

Books By Sunni T. Connor

- DAMAGED little girl
- A DAMAGED WOMAN
- DAMIEN'S SECRET
- DAMIEN'S SECRET II
- Niña Dañada (Spanish version of DAMAGED little girl)

Stay In Contact

www.naturallysunni.com
IG: Sunni_theauthor
FB: Sunni Connor
YT: Naturally Sunni